# SWEET MEANT TO BE

## BARBARA MCMAHON

# Chapter One

"I know he said the place was located in a pristine wilderness, but this is ridiculous!" Dani Winthrop mumbled aloud as her car continued to barrel and bounce along the gravel road. She hadn't seen another vehicle heading in either direction since she'd left the small town of Carson Creek, Colorado, forty minutes ago.

"If they don't do some serious improvement to this road, they'll never have repeat guests," she grumbled. "First time guests might turn around halfway. Especially in winter." Which is exactly what she was tempted to do.

The car bumped and skidded, gravel spewing. She fought the wheel to keep the car straight.

The road had obviously been graded at some point— obviously with a load of gravel. But it was already showing ruts from heavy traffic. She didn't even want to speculate what it would be like in rain or a snowstorm. Thank heaven for good weather.

She gripped the steering wheel tighter, easing up on the accelerator.

"Hang on, babykins, it can't be that much farther. He said thirty miles from town, and we've gone at least that." She wished she'd checked the odometer when she turned off the highway. It seemed as if she'd been traveling all day.

Six months pregnant, Dani constantly talked to her baby. She'd read somewhere that children recognized their mother's voice from their time in the womb. So she talked frequently, wanting her infant to know her from the first moment. To know she loved him or her completely no matter what happened. That she was a mother to be counted on, and she would never desert her child—not as her father had. Or her mother. Or her baby's father.

"At least I think it can't be much farther," she murmured, peering into the distance. It wasn't an easy feat with soaring lodge pole pines lining both sides of the road. The long-range view was where the road cut a swath through the tall timber as it crested a hill. Beyond was the endless blue of a clear autumn sky.

She felt a hint of trepidation as she surveyed the wilderness, but pushed it away. She needed this job. It had sounded perfect when she'd first learned about it in the employment agency in Denver—a temporary secretary's position for two months. One that paid almost twice what she'd been earning in the city, with accommodations included. It would tap into her expertise in the building industry, as well. It was the perfect job, even if it was clear across the state from where she lived.

The remote construction site would be in operation only another six to eight weeks before winter closed in and made further work impossible until next spring.

The timing had been perfect. Getting away from Denver had seemed ideal when she first considered the job.

But now reality began to seep in.

Carson Creek was a quaint little mountain town, with one main street and two secondary streets lined with small shops and businesses—and the county's only hospital.

Dani couldn't ignore medical facilities. Not that she expected to need them. She had plenty of time to decide where to settle into a new place before the baby was due.

But it didn't hurt to know where the nearest medical assistance was—just in case.

"I sure hope it's not much farther, because if I don't find that construction site soon, I'll have to find a convenient tree!"

One of the definite down sides to pregnancy was the frequent need for restroom facilities—which weren't available along the side of *this* excuse for a road.

Cresting a hill a few moments later, Dani slowed, a smile lighting her features. "Hallelujah! Bathroom here we come."

Spread before her was the construction site she'd traveled two hundred miles to reach. Making her way down the sweep of gravel road, she tried to take in everything, from the tall crane swinging a long piling into place, to the heavy earth movers parked on the far side of the mammoth clearing, to the sparkling water of the high Alpine lake, part of the spectacular view beyond.

To the left, a hodgepodge of trailers and campers lined the perimeter of the cleared area, with cars and trucks interspersed. Trees surrounded the site, dark green and soaring taller than any she'd seen before. But the jewel was the deep blue Alpine lake, pristine and clear, and stretching as far as the eye could see.

Dani took a deep breath as she eased her car down the hill. Once the road was paved, the thirty-mile trip from Carson Creek could be made in half the time it'd taken her. And it would be a lot smoother. Her hands ached from fighting the steering. Her teeth had been rattled more than enough.

"We're almost there," she murmured, searching for which trailer was most likely the office.

She'd check in, find out which trailer had been allocated for her use, and move in her few belongings. It wouldn't take long to get settled.

She especially wanted to refrigerate the groceries she'd bought in Carson Creek before they spoiled.

And she wanted a bathroom in the worst way.

She spotted a trailer apart from the others, nearer the work site, and headed for it. It had to be the office. All around her men worked in precision as they toiled to create a luxury resort in the Colorado wilderness. Hard hats gleamed in the sun. The drone of the crane as it swung the piling into place was background noise to the bang of hammers, the whine of a drill and the buzz of power saws.

Dani pulled to a stop by the office. She hastened out of her car and walked quickly up the two steps into the trailer, excitement bubbling inside her.

"Dani Winthrop! You made it!" Mick Flannagan rose from behind one of three battered desks. A tall man with a shock of gray hair, he held out his hand. He'd been the one to interview her and offer her the job back in Denver.

Grateful for the friendly welcome, she felt some of her worry fade. Dani smiled and took his hand. "Your directions were excellent."

"You made good time. I didn't expect you before dark."

"I didn't want to risk driving after sundown on an unfamiliar road. Especially one that isn't paved. Carson Creek looks like a darling town. I stocked up on groceries before I left."

She planned to visit on her days off—explore the small shops, eat at the local café, surround herself with some civilization, quiet though it might be.

"It's the closest place for R and R we have when not

working. Of course, it's not up to Denver's standards. Come on over and have a seat."

"Uh, maybe I could freshen up first?"

"Go right down that short hall. Take your time. When you're ready, I'll show you around. Get you settled."

"Thanks."

Dani almost flew down the hall, her long, flowing dress snapping around her legs. She was most comfortable these days in loose-fitting cotton dresses. The pink one she wore now gathered beneath her breasts, the full skirt hitting her mid calf. It swayed when she walked, billowing out behind her as she hurried. It also camouflaged most signs of pregnancy, not that she could be called svelte by any means. But the major growth of her baby was yet to come.

She suddenly wondered how suitable dresses would be on a construction site. It hadn't been a problem in the offices in Denver, but this was definitely not Denver. Still, it wasn't as if she'd be climbing girders or hammering nails.

Dani was washing her hands when she felt the trailer move slightly, felt a vibration of the floor. Someone had joined Mick. Was it his partner?

She knew from her interview that Mick and a man named Connor Norris had been business partners for several years. And that this was their biggest project to date—and in danger of falling behind because of paperwork snafus.

Not to mention that their previous secretary had quit abruptly, leaving everything in chaos.

Dani hadn't figured out why the secretary had left. Mick had been quite vague about that, and Dani hadn't felt it was her place to ask. Now that she was here, and a part of the team, maybe she'd be clued in.

She checked her appearance in the mirror. There wasn't much she could do about the wild mop of blond curls. They were as tamed as they got. Touching up her pink lipstick, she smiled. Hoping to make as good an impression on Connor Norris as she had with Mick, she opened the door and headed back down the short hall. She heard voices and took a deep breath, ready to meet whomever had arrived.

"I saw the car, wanted to meet the new man. There's no emergency on the site." A strong voice carried to her ears.

"I can get the new secretary settled in."

That was Mick's voice. Did it sound a bit hesitant Dani wondered.

"Hey, he made good time. There're a few hours left until quitting time. Maybe he can make some headway in that stack of permits today. If we don't get caught up soon, the entire project's going to fall behind schedule, and that's something I don't plan to allow!"

Dani stepped into the doorway. The man who stood casually beside Mick's desk, leafing through a stack of mail, was tall, dark, and seethed with impatience.

Dani blinked. She was five feet two herself, so most men seemed to tower above her. This one had to be six feet tall, with shoulders a yard wide. His T-shirt had the sleeves ripped out, and the rippling muscles covered by taut, tanned skin had her admiring superb musculature. Undoubtedly from hard physical labor. No gym could produce such bronzed skin, defined muscles and the air of command emanating from him even as he glanced through a handful of envelopes.

He caught her movement and looked up. His eyes were dark and unfathomable, but a hint of shock showed. Then they narrowed as he studied her. He looked at Mick, raising an eyebrow in silent inquiry.

The older man shrugged. "I didn't get around to telling you—our new secretary is a she."

"What! *You didn't get around to telling me?* You hired her last week! You've been back here four days. I can't believe this! Mick, have you gone crazy? The last thing we need around here is a woman. We have fifty-three men working flat out and we need everyone to concentrate on their job, not slack off trying to make time with some blonde! Who knows how much longer we have before the weather turns? Get rid of her!"

He tossed the papers on the desk and strode out of the office without looking at Dani again. The door slammed, the sound reverberating in the narrow confines of the trailer.

"Gee, that went well," Dani said. She looked at Mick. "Who was that?"

A niggling worry had her guessing exactly who he was.

"That's my partner, Connor Norris." Mick smiled wryly. "His bark's worse than his bite. He'll come around."

"I gave up my job, my apartment, and put almost everything I own into storage to come to this job," Dani said, that hint of trepidation she'd felt earlier expanding, engulfing her.

She'd been thrilled to get the position, especially because it was so far from Denver. So thrilled, she'd lost no time in rearranging her life and burning her bridges behind her. If she lost the position before she began, what would she do?

*She needed this job!*

Mick rose. "Don't worry about a thing. Connor'll come around. You're staying. This'll be your desk." He indicated the one near the window—piled with stacks of folders, unopened mail and rolled-up blueprints. Some of the clutter spilled over onto the chair, the wide windowsill behind it and the floor.

Had anything been done since the former secretary left?

Exactly how long had she—no, undoubtedly *he*—been gone?

"Connor was right about one thing, though, we need to get going with this paper mess to make sure we stay on target. Pete left us in the lurch when he took off unexpectedly like he did." Mick looked at her sharply. "I know we discussed timing—two months minimum—but we need to make sure you plan to stay until we shut down for the winter. We need all the paperwork caught up."

"I'm not going anywhere," Dani said, walking over to the desk to look at the different stacks.

She was curious about Connor, longed to ask questions about the other partner. How much weight did he carry? Would he try to run her off? Was Mick able to guarantee she could stay?

Was there more to Connor Norris's dislike of her than the fact that she was female? Surely Mick would have taken that into consideration before offering her the job.

And get real—who was going to try to make time with a woman six months pregnant? His workers' concentration was safe.

She wasn't scheduled to start work until tomorrow. Not that she would let that stop her. But first–

"I'd like to put away my groceries. I have some things that need to go into the refrigerator," Dani said, turning away from the desk. "Then I can begin."

"Tomorrow's soon enough," Mick said easily.

Dani studied him a moment.

The contrast between the two men was extensive based on what she'd observed so far. But she'd do better to err on the side of caution.

"I think it best if I get started today. Sort things out if nothing else."

And dig in, hoping to make a place for herself so Mr. Get-Rid-of-Her had to eat his words!

He nodded. "Don't take Connor's comment to heart. He's a hard man. But as long as you do the job, he'll come around. Come on, I'll show you the trailer. It's the third one in line, next to mine."

When they reached Dani's car, Mick nodded toward the row of trailers and campers. "Most of the men stay on-site. A few drive back and forth to town each night. You can park on the far side of the silver trailer."

He crossed the road while she started her car and drove slowly to the trailer indicated. She looked down the long row, wondering how much the command Connor had issued should concern her.

While she couldn't help anyone else's behavior, Connor had nothing to worry about from her end. She wouldn't encourage flirting. The last thing she wanted was any involvement with another man. Or anyone else, for that matter.

She had few friends, but that was by choice. If she didn't let people get close, then she wouldn't be hurt when they disappointed her.

She'd been such a fool to trust Marc. Getting involved with him had broken one of her staunchest rules—never date co-workers.

She'd learned that lesson well. Never again!

"One would think," she said aloud, "that after twenty-seven years of being abandoned, let down and disappointed, one would learn. But oh, no, I had to fall for Marc's blue eyes and fancy compliments. Let that be a lesson to you, babykins."

The baby kicked and Dani smiled, rubbing her stomach gently, her heart swelling with love. "It's you and me, kid. But we'll do great!"

Dani looked on the new job as a positive sign. She'd been miserable the last four months at her job in Denver, in the building department where Marc worked as an inspector. Running into each other from time to time was unavoidable. He had totally ignored her since she'd refused to get an abortion. In fact, he seemed to make more of a point to flirt with other women when she was around.

She hadn't been able to turn off her feelings as easily as he had, though by the end of the third week of his rejection, she had grown contemptuous and then angry.

Had he had any genuine feelings for her to begin with? She'd once thought he hung the moon. How quickly that illusion shattered.

She tried to shake off the feelings of inadequacy that plagued her whenever she thought of that last scene with Marc. He hadn't wanted anything to do with her or their baby. A wife and child had no place in his plans for life.

Had that been how her own father felt? Was it a man's instinctive reaction to being tied down, to being responsible for another life? Her parents had never married. Once her father discovered a baby was on the way, he'd taken off.

Dani could still vaguely remember her mother complaining, before she herself dumped Dani with social services one day and took off. Dani had been about five, but still remembered how lost she felt and how scared.

Yet she saw families all the time—happy families. Fathers who seemed to love their wives and children. Who laughed and smiled during shopping trips to the mall or outings in the park.

Even at the building department, some men kept pictures of their families on their desks, had love shining on their faces as they joked about babies teething or keeping them awake walking the floor with them in the night.

The happy family scene seemed to escape Dani. She'd never mastered it when she was a child, nor found it as an adult.

Now she planned a new direction.

The prospect of a good, well-paying job on a site two hundred miles from Denver had given her new hope for the future—a future she planned to build for herself and her child.

No more ventures into romance; no more trying to fit in with other people's plans and goals. She would depend on no one but herself. She would make her own decisions and be independent.

The salary offered proved to be much higher than what she'd been earning—higher than usual to attract and hold good workers, the employment agency had told her.

There weren't a lot of amenities. The nearest town was thirty miles away. Nonetheless, the job had seemed heaven-sent, to Dani. She'd mind her own business, keep to herself and save her money like crazy.

As she parked her car, she vowed she'd prove herself to Mick—and Connor. They didn't have to worry about their fifty-three other employees. She was here to work and get on with her life, not be a distraction.


Connor glared at Moose Higgins. The man was one talented crane operator—except when he stopped paying attention.

"That's the fourth time I've told you to watch the edge of the cleared space. You just missed whacking those trees. I can't afford to have that crane go out of commission. We're already almost a week behind."

"Hey, boss, lighten up. I didn't hit anything. Came close, but close only counts in horseshoes."

Connor wasn't appeased. "Don't do it again."

Moose shrugged and put the heavy crane into slow motion. He was as big as his name implied, but handled the heavy equipment with the delicate skill of a surgeon.

It wasn't Moose's fault, Connor reluctantly admitted as he watched the skillful man maneuver the huge machine, beginning the intricate process of moving a twenty-five-foot beam into place.

The fault was his.

He was angry at Mick and taking it out on Moose. What had his partner been thinking? They were behind on the site work, behind on the paperwork, and already out several thousand dollars, thanks to Pete's embezzlement. To top things off, Mick had to go hire a petite, feminine *woman!*

It was already September. Before long, the winter snow would start falling, forcing them into a hiatus until spring.

He needed someone who could unjam the logjam, seriously kick some butt to get the local officials off their collective duffs to grant their building approvals.

Not some blonde who looked as if a strong wind would knock her over.

This was a hard-core construction site. Men responded to men. Not to some petite blonde with wide blue eyes, dressed in gauzy pink dresses.

Leave it to Mick to be attracted to a pretty face, hear a sob story and offer her a job, her performance of which would undoubtedly set them back even more.

Connor didn't have time to interview a bunch of people himself. He was needed on-site. Mick knew that. It was the reason he'd been charged with hiring someone while on the buying trip to Denver.

Had he gone crazy, or just been bowled over by bright blue eyes?

Connor scowled.

Blue eyes were blue eyes. He was lucky he'd even noticed the color. She was too young, too small, too feminine to work on a construction site.

He tried to ignore the face that seemed to dance before him as he watched Moose swing the beam. Her sunny smile had dimmed when he'd told Mick to get rid of her. Her shoulders had slumped slightly for a moment, then straightened up as if she were ready for battle.

Connor gave a cursory glance around and headed back to the office. There wasn't going to be a battle. He'd told Mick to send her packing.

End of discussion.

Now it'd be at least another week before he could interview anyone. He'd better go through the pile on the secretary's desk himself and see what he could handle. Paperwork was not a part of the job he liked, but he'd do it if he had to.

And Mick could do more himself.

It wasn't that his partner didn't pull his weight, but lately Mick—

Opening the door, Connor frowned when he saw that the trailer was empty, the phone ringing off the hook. Where was Mick?

Connor snatched up the phone and looked out the window.

"Norris," he said curtly.

He saw the woman's car parked beside the third trailer. What was she doing here? And by the empty trailer?

An uneasy thought sprang to mind. No! Mick wouldn't—

"Norris, Barton here. We've run into a snafu with your latest lumber order," the voice on the other end said.

Connor switched gears. He'd deal with the secretary situation after he settled with Miles Barton about the latest problem.

# Chapter Two

"This'll do fine." Dani looked around the small trailer. It was like a tiny apartment. The living room segued into a dining nook and galley kitchen. The hallway mimicked the one in the office, leading to a bed and bath.

From one window, she saw the trailer next door. From the back, however, she had a stunning view of the tall trees and the mountains rising majestically around her. And even a sliver of the lake.

Best of all, it was free—part of the compensation package. And she still got a healthy salary—how lucky could she be?

Mick's partner was not driving her away from this job!

"I know it's far from the city and all. In your condition, you sure you'll be okay here? The trailers don't have phones, but I'm right next door. And we agreed we'll be shutting down operations for the winter long before you'd start your maternity leave," Mick said, sounding worried.

Dani nodded, wanting to pat Mick's arm and reassure him she was fine. She wasn't used to people taking such an interest and showing so much concern in her life. She'd been on her own since she turned eighteen—nine years ago. It was sweet, but not something she'd grow to expect—or trust.

He was her boss. One of her bosses.

And she knew enough not to step over that line.

"This will suit me perfectly."

"I'll bring in your things."

She swiftly put away the perishables, while Mick helped her put away canned goods and packages. He carried her suitcases and two cardboard boxes into her bedroom.

"I'll unpack later," Dani told him.

She didn't want help unpacking. Or in anything else. The less she depended upon others, the less likely she was to be disappointed when they walked away.

"I'm anxious to get started on the job."

"Don't you want to rest up after your trip?" he asked.

"Not necessary. I did nothing but drive, which meant sitting the entire way. Now I'd like to get to work. That's what you're paying me for."

And she didn't want to provide any reason for his partner to fire her. Despite what Connor said, she'd come to this job in good faith. He couldn't fire her merely for being a woman.

Only if she messed up. Which she didn't plan to do.

Mick handed her a key as they left the trailer. He watched as Dani carefully locked her door.

"It's not that we have a lot of crime here," he said when they began walking toward the office, "but with all the men around, you'll need to be a bit careful. Some of these guys are mavericks."

"I'll keep to myself," she said. She wasn't looking for anyone coming to visit. She wanted time alone and expected to get it.

"Up to walking?" he asked.

"Sure."

She smiled, wondering how to set Mick straight. It couldn't be more than a hundred yards to the office.

"I'm pregnant, not sick. Walking is good exercise. I usually do a couple of miles a day."

"Not many places to walk around here."

"Are you kidding? There are hundreds of acres of pristine forest land. Not to mention the shore of the lake. I can't wait to explore that. And if I want a longer ramble, I can always walk back up the road a piece."

"Not in your condition." He looked appalled.

"I'm fine, Mick."

She wouldn't allow him to think she couldn't manage on her own. Even if his motives were sincere, she liked her independence. Depending on others always let her down.

Besides, she didn't dare let him think she was too fragile to do the job. She needed him on her side if it came to a showdown with his partner.

When Dani stepped into the office, the first thing she saw was Connor rummaging through the stacks of papers on her desk. Her heart skipped a beat. He looked rugged and focused.

Quite a contrast to Marc's rather dapper dress. He hated the times he had to inspect the early stages of buildings, especially if the weather was inclement.

Dani had no difficulty picturing this man out in any and all types of weather, relishing the challenges of nature, defying odds to bring the project in on schedule. While only an inch or two taller than Marc, Connor radiated a power that the other man would only envy.

"Can I help you find something?" she asked calmly.

She knew enough about psychology to know that it would be best to keep any hint of worry from showing.

He turned and looked at her. For a moment Dani felt a frisson of apprehension. He appeared angry. Or was that scowl his perpetual expression?

"Why are you still here? We'll pay for your travel time and any inconvenience we caused. You might want to take off before it gets dark."

"There's been no inconvenience. I've come to work and I'll do my job."

She walked behind the desk and sat down defiantly, almost holding her breath as she threw out the challenge.

Mick remained by the door—in order to make a quick escape Dani wondered.

"Are you *pregnant?*" Connor asked in disbelief, staring at her stomach.

Had he not noticed earlier?

"Almost six months. Don't worry, it's not contagious. And it doesn't interfere with my abilities."

He swung around to Mick.

"You hired a *pregnant woman* to come out here? I don't believe this! Have you lost what little mind you had left?"

"She's got experience in the building industry. Her skills are great. She'll be able to do a lot to help out without our having to teach her every step. She'll be doing office work, not heavy construction. Besides, it wasn't as if we had a lot of choice. People aren't exactly champing at the bit to come to some construction site thirty miles from the nearest town—even for a couple of months. I figured any help was better than coming back empty-handed."

Dani looked at Mick in dismay. She'd been sure her experience had impressed him, that he'd truly thought she was the best person for the job. The pride she'd felt in landing the position deflated.

Standing suddenly, she tilted her head pugnaciously.

"Give me a week. If you aren't totally satisfied with all I've done, I'll leave and you won't even have to pay me for the week," she said before she could think.

Connor looked at her, frowning.

Mick looked at her, frowning.

"No."

Connor's flat-out denial was immediate; no compromise from him. His dark eyes sent a shiver coursing down her back. Dani wanted more than anything to prove to him she could do the job—to have him change his mind and eat crow.

"That's not fair to you, Dani," Mick protested.

"I think it's fair. Especially if you *are* satisfied with my work, I stay and you give me a bonus."

It was a gamble, but she was desperate. Her gaze locked with Connor's while endless moments ticked by. He was the one to convince.

"Today is Tuesday. You have until Friday. Then you're gone," Connor said, breaking eye contact first.

He turned and glared at Mick. "And I'll do the interviewing next time."

"Won't be a next time," Dani muttered, already delving into the stack of rolled-up blueprints.

She continued to sort and stack the various documents on her desk, almost holding her breath until the two men left. Then with a whoosh, she let it out, leaning back in her chair and gazing around her in dismay.

What had she so recklessly done? She'd be lucky to find her way around the office by Friday, much less prove to be invaluable to a man whose mind was made up that she was expendable.

She needed the money. How foolish to say they needn't pay

her. Her primary reason for accepting a job so far away from everything she knew was the added pay. She didn't have much in savings, though she'd been scrimping to augment what she had ever since she'd discovered she was pregnant.

Ever since she'd learned Marc wanted nothing further to do with her or their child.

Something about Connor got her back up and gave her a new focus. She wanted him to turn around and admit she was suitable for the job. It was personal now.

The baby kicked and Dani idly rubbed her stomach. "Buckle up, babykins, we're in for a bumpy ride!"

The phone rang and Dani answered it. Her job had begun in earnest.

By the time Dani's stomach had growled for the third time, she was ready to call it a day. Glancing out the window, she noticed all was quiet on the job site. The noise from the heavy machinery had faded long ago. The sound of hammers ringing and the buzz of the saws had ended without her noticing.

She surveyed her desk with quiet satisfaction. She'd gone through everything and sorted it into piles. She had fielded calls, settled one problem with a vendor and been the target of curious construction workers who had found one dumb excuse after another to stop into the office during the afternoon.

Mick had been there most of the time. She'd done her best to ignore the visitors, claiming she hadn't a clue yet where things were when they asked, and suggesting they talk to Connor.

She'd love to know if any had followed through. She could just imagine what Connor would have said to any man who mentioned he'd talked with her!

Though she hoped none were crazy enough to ask him. She didn't want anyone giving credence to his prediction about her being a distraction.

Dani walked outside, locking the door behind her. The fresh air was pleasant, though cool. The sun had already moved behind the ridge, bathing the valley in deep shadows.

When she drew near her trailer, her relief was almost tangible. She was on her own until eight the next morning.

The door of the first trailer opened and Connor stepped out. His eyes narrowed as he saw her, but he said nothing, walking on down the beaten path toward the lake as if she hadn't been there.

She tossed her head. She didn't care. He could be as rude as he liked when they weren't working. It was only for two months and she could stand anything for that long.

Tonight she'd unpack, take a soothing bath and fix something light for dinner. Then it was bed for her! She'd read until she fell asleep. It had been a long day.

Connor knew trouble in the making. It was bad enough having Dani Winthrop work here, but Mick had to make it convenient for her to stay on-site. The whole setup was explosive. He only hoped he could stave it off until she left on Friday.

Connor headed for the lake and the quiet spot he liked to find at the end of the day.

One of the trailers had lights on inside. It wasn't dark, but the sun had already slipped behind the high peaks to the west. Twilight fell early in the high country in late September.

He liked this time of day. He always had. He and his late wife, Catherine.

As he walked to the lake's edge, he heard the drone of television coming from a couple of trailers, ribald conversation from another. A small group of guys sat in folding chairs near one camper, swapping stories. When Connor reached the lake, he nodded to a couple of men trying their hand at fishing.

They were building a luxury resort for the Windhaven Corporation in the middle of the Colorado wilderness. The lake was one of the major attractions. The proximity to cross-country ski resorts and hunting and fishing were aspects the corporation planned to highlight. As well as a state-of-the-art spa to attract women.

For a place to relax, it wouldn't be beat. Connor knew the resort would charge guests an arm and a leg, and visitors would happily pay for the remote luxury and pristine setting.

He'd be long gone by then. To another site, another job. Another couple of years in a remote location. Getting through life one day at a time.

He walked along the edge of the lake, stopping at a tree that had fallen partially into the water. Placing a foot on the trunk, he rested his elbow against his knee and took a swig of the cold soft drink he'd carried.

He was alone and liked it that way.

Catherine would have loved this place, he thought for the hundredth time.

The familiar ache took hold.

He always missed her, but especially at twilight. They'd made it a tradition to have a quiet drink together, just the two of them, before dinner every evening. Even after Sammy had come along, it had been their special time to talk over their respective days, and to be with each other. To shut out the rest of the world and draw their own world around them.

He gripped the can tightly. The ache would get worse as the night wore on. It had been three years, but it could have been three minutes or three decades. With his wife gone it was like a part of himself had been amputated.

Which it had—the best part of him.

He could close his eyes and see her—tall and slim with dark eyes and sleek dark hair that framed her face. She'd been almost as tall as he was when she'd worn high heels. They'd known each other since fourth grade. Their likes had meshed; their thoughts had run parallel. Their dreams had been the same.

He rubbed his chest, the ache was impossible. Some days he thought he couldn't make it without her.

Her and Sammy.

If he closed his eyes, he could see her walking toward him. Hear her sweet voice—

"Mr. Norris, there's a problem with my water. I can't find Mick. Can you fix it?"

Connor opened his eyes and turned.

Instead of Catherine's tall dark beauty, he confronted the petite blonde Mick had hired. The petite, *pregnant* blonde who barely came up to his shoulder.

Irritation rose. What did she want now? If she thought he planned to baby-sit her until Friday, she had another thought coming.

He still didn't know why he'd given her until Friday. She should have headed back to Carson Creek already.

# Chapter Three

"What do you want?"

"Someone to fix the water in my trailer. I knocked on Mick's door. He said he has the trailer next door to mine, but he's not there. And I don't know anyone else to ask. I certainly don't want you to think I was *flirting* with someone if I asked for assistance," Dani said.

Connor took another swallow of the soda, his cherished quiet shattered. He scanned her from head to toe, irritated anew at the sight of her. The asperity in her voice was noticeable.

He straightened. She was right; if there was a problem, he or Mick should fix it. No sense opening a crack in a door for any of the men to think it was an invitation.

"What's wrong with the water?"

"I can't get any hot. It comes out cold from both faucets. There's a hot-water heater, but I don't know a thing about it and don't know if it's working properly."

"Probably needs a new propane tank hooked up."

She stared at him. Her eyes were darker in the twilight—not deep brown as Catherine's had been, but navy blue.

Navy blue eyes? It had to be lack of light or altitude sickness. What was wrong with him? She had plain old blue eyes, period.

He sighed over the inevitable and turned to begin to walk back along the shore, then up the slight incline, heading toward the trailers. Despite not wanting her around, he'd fix the blasted hot-water heater. A pregnant woman needed warm water.

A shaft of pain pierced him. He remembered how much Catherine had liked soaking in hot baths when she'd been pregnant with Sammy. Sometimes he'd joined her, the two of them sloshing water everywhere.

Quickening his pace, he tried to put distance between him and the memories. It took a couple of minutes to realize Dani Winthrop was almost running to keep up with him.

Connor stopped abruptly. She skidded to a halt and looked at him, her breasts rising and falling rapidly as she tried to catch her breath. The higher elevation took some getting used to. Exertion wasn't recommended until a person had become acclimated.

"You needn't run," he said.

"I want to see how you fix the hot-water heater. If there's a problem in the future, I can take care of it myself if I know how."

"There won't be another problem before Friday."

She tilted her chin, meeting his gaze. "I meant beyond Friday—when I'm still here and a valuable member of the team!"

Connor felt a twitch of amusement.

He'd give her credit for being tenacious, if nothing else. But the proof would be in the work and the way she handled herself. He didn't have time for dilettantes. Tomorrow he'd make sure she realized fully what all was involved. He'd bet she'd be gone by sundown.

He turned back toward her trailer, moving more slowly,

conscious of the woman beside him. He'd never had to shorten his stride with Catherine.

As they walked along, Connor's senses were teased by the floral scent that seemed to float around Dani Winthrop. It was light and delicate—like she was. It brought home how much he'd missed a woman's presence in the last three years. And how long the years stretched out empty and lonely ahead of him.

Unable to bear the reality of Catherine's and Sammy's deaths, he'd thrown himself into his work, taking on more and more. Joining Mick in partnership, he 'd pushed to build their newly formed J&J Construction to the size it was today. He didn't have time for friendships beyond the job site, and had no plans to ever get involved with another woman.

One heartache in this lifetime was more than he could handle.

Yet for the first time in three years, he was actually looking at a woman. Smelling her scent. Speculating about the true color of her eyes.

And wishing she were a hundred miles away.

Innocently walking beside him, Dani obviously hadn't a clue about the turmoil he felt. The sooner he got her hot-water heater fixed, the sooner she'd be closed up in her trailer and out of sight—and scent. He didn't need her to remind him of all he'd lost.

It took five minutes to locate a new propane tank, hook it to the hot-water heater and ignite the pilot light. Once he heard the whoosh that indicated the heater was working, he turned and almost crashed into her. Dani had been at his elbow every step of the way, watching closely as he worked, asking intelligent questions.

She stepped back quickly, a hint of worry in her eyes.

"It'll take a while for the water to heat," he said, wanting to step back, to put distance between them. But the close confines of the trailer didn't allow that luxury. Why didn't she move?

"I know. I'll eat dinner first. Then take a quick shower." She sighed softly. "I had hoped for a nice hot bath, but a shower is all this place has."

She smiled politely and stepped back into the living area of the trailer.

Connor followed, intent on leaving before he did something else stupid.

He had a tub in his trailer—the only one in camp, if he remembered correctly. For an instant he almost offered her the use of it.

Then sanity took hold. He didn't want her here and didn't plan to do anything to encourage her staying. By Friday, she'd have to admit defeat and depart.

And if life wasn't as comfortable as she'd hoped, maybe she'd leave even earlier.

"We start work at eight," he said gruffly, feeling a hint of guilt for denying her such a minor bit of comfort. But he was determined to have her gone in three days.

"I'll be there. Thank you for fixing the heater."

She ushered him to the door and practically shut it in his face.

He stood on the step for a moment, surprised by her move. *What did you expect?* he asked himself as he walked away. He'd done nothing since they'd met to encourage any friendly feelings.

Still, he admitted he'd expected her to try to change his mind—with a smile, or soft words, or an invitation for a drink.

The fact that she hadn't surprised him.

Dani stood beneath the hot shower some time later and

reveled in the warmth. She wished she could have had a nice soak, but the water felt almost as good cascading down as it would sitting in it. Tilting back her head, she wet her hair, relishing the feeling. She wished the lake was warm enough to swim in—not that late September was the time to go swimming in Colorado's high country. The lake was probably icy cold even in summer. But it had looked inviting.

When the water began to turn cool, she shut it off and stepped out into the minuscule bathroom. It didn't take long to dry off and don the flannel nightie she'd brought. Nights were cool in Denver and she'd known they would be cold in the mountains. Combing her hair, she debated using a dryer. Her hair would curl in any case, so she might as well let it dry naturally.

Slipping beneath the covers a little while later, she turned off the light without reading. She wanted to get a good night's sleep. She had a feeling she'd need all her wits about her tomorrow to prove to at least one critical partner that she was the perfect secretary.

Curiously, she had no doubt that if she proved her worth, Connor would let her stay until they closed down for the winter. She suspected he was an honorable man, a man of his word.

She grinned in the darkness. He hadn't wanted to help her tonight. But he had. Without a word of complaint. Another man might have said that was one hardship of working on a remote site—that they all dealt with cold showers—as a way to discourage her. But he hadn't.

He'd been patient in answering her questions, too, though he was convinced she'd never need a working knowledge of the heater or propane tank.

Would he graciously accept defeat when she showed him

she could stay the course?

Or would he always be looking for fault, searching for any excuse to fire her and get rid of the woman secretary? He'd agreed to the outrageous terms she'd flung out. If she passed, she'd stay. Something about the man told her that.

But he was the one who'd decide if she passed, and she knew the deck was stacked against her.

Dani was already on the phone to the county building department when Connor entered the trailer the next morning. She'd seen him up on the framework of the main building when she'd crossed to the office, but he hadn't seen her. He'd been deep in conversation with two other men, comfortably at home on the high skeleton of the new resort.

How long had he worked in construction? Probably since he was a teenager, to be so comfortable on precarious structures.

He looked at her with surprise when he entered.

"It's only a few minutes past eight o'clock. If he could be here by one, that would work," she said to the woman on the other end of the line.

Dani tried to focus on the conversation at hand, ignoring Connor's presence to the best of her abilities.

But something about him sparked an awareness she wasn't used to. It was as if the air shimmered with static electricity in his presence.

She almost grinned at her frivolous thoughts. If there were electricity present, he'd use it to zap her away.

Dani smiled in triumph, but let none of her jubilation show in her voice when the woman on the other end acquiesced.

"Thank you, I'll let them know he'll be here by one."

She hung up the phone.

"That was?" Connor asked, leaning against the edge of his desk, his focus on her. His dark eyes were narrowed, offering no clue to his feelings, yet the intensity was disconcerting.

Dani felt almost as if he touched her. A tangible awareness seemed to grow. Shivering slightly, she tried to ignore her reactions and smiled in delight.

"The county building department. You'll have an inspector here by one."

She wanted to jump up and dance around in triumph, but contained her excitement. Mick had told her how frustrated they'd been with inspection delays. Let Connor think it was all in a day's work for someone with her expertise. A few more triumphs like that and he'd have to admit she was more than suitable—she was indispensable!

"And just how did you manage that feat?" His eyes never left hers as he awaited her answer.

"Knowing who to contact and how to apply the right pressure."

And a lot of luck, but he didn't have to know that part.

He stared at her for a long moment.

Dani caught her breath, held it as her heart rate sped up exponentially. She couldn't look away, couldn't break eye contact, could only gaze into those dark eyes that gave nothing away. What was he thinking? Did he feel any of the shimmering tension that seemed to fill the office trailer?

Abruptly, he nodded once and moved to sit behind his desk. The phone rang and he snatched it up.

She glanced away, slowly letting her breath out and taking another.

What had just happened?

She drew a line through that item on her to-do list, trying to focus on all she had to accomplish and not on the other occupant of the office. Getting the inspector out on such short notice was a small victory in the greater scheme of things, but it definitely didn't hurt that Mr. Doubting Thomas over there had witnessed it.

Chalk one up for her side.

Now if she could only ignore him and the strange reactions she experienced, maybe she could get something else crossed off her lengthy list.

Despite the edge of tension that seemed to permeate the office during the morning, Dani was able to accomplish a great deal. Yet even as she diligently worked through the backed-up paperwork, she was conscious of Connor more than she should have been.

The way he ran his fingers through that thick hair had nothing to do with anything and she had no business noting the gesture each time he made it. His hair was almost black and thick. When he ran his fingers through it, it looked mussed. Intriguing.

She blinked and stared back at her notes. Don't go there!

The sound of his deep voice when speaking on the phone did not send shivers down her back. That was the draft from the door, she tried to convince herself.

When he frowned at something, she was glad that glare wasn't directed at her—her heart rate picked up, anyway.

And she wondered what he'd look like if he smiled or laughed.

Mick joined them at ten, after reviewing plans with one of the masons on the far side of the site. His presence eased the tension a notch or two. Maybe with a third person there, her wild imagination would ease up and she could get more accomplished.

Dani couldn't completely relax. She was too aware on a sensual level of the man at the adjacent desk.

Did Connor normally stay in the office all day? Wasn't he needed on the construction site to oversee something? Had he only stayed in the office today to keep an eye on her—hoping to find fault and get rid of her even earlier than Friday?

She'd go crazy if he spent eight hours a day, every day, in such close proximity.

"It's after twelve. When do you plan to eat lunch?" Connor said unexpectedly.

Dani looked up from the stack of invoices she was trying to put in order. She glanced at her watch. The morning had flown by.

"Is this the normal lunch hour?"

He nodded.

Silence outside indicated the men had stopped work.

She rose, smoothing her dark blue dress and taking her purse. "I'll be back at one, then."

"If I'm not here, follow up on these calls, will you?" he asked, holding out a small stack of pink telephone messages.

"Certainly."

Mick smiled, keeping his face down as if studying the blueprints spread across his desk.

Connor glanced at him. "Something funny?"

His partner looked up and shook his head. "Thought you didn't want Dani here. You delegating work to her now?"

"If she were staying, she'd need to be able to handle the office when you and I aren't here. Might as well see how she shapes up while we're still around."

A hint of exhilaration swept through Dani as she walked back to her trailer.

Was Connor thawing, as Mick had predicted? One gesture wasn't enough to judge. A cordial word or two would help. Was he as gruff with all his employees? Maybe he wasn't used to being around a woman.

Not that she wanted special consideration.

After she prepared her lunch, she sat down on the sofa and put her feet up on a chair. Leaning back, she enjoyed being able to totally relax. She was tired—not that she'd admit that to her boss. She'd give anything if she could take a short nap.

# Chapter Four

Instead, she nibbled on her tuna sandwich, idly speculating about the taciturn Mr. Norris.

He seemed a hard man, with definite opinions and not much give in him. How had he and easygoing Mick ever hooked up? He was years younger than Mick, in his early thirties, she'd guess, while Mick had to be in his mid-to late fifties.

Did Connor ever smile? She hadn't seen him do so yet. Not that they'd spent that much time together. And, truth to tell, she didn't mind if they didn't spend any more time together. Until she could convince him she was the best person for the job–he was the enemy.

Ordinarily, she'd be pleased with what she'd accomplished with little direction on her first day. Still, she knew it might not be enough to suit him. He had the final say. But she'd go down fighting every inch of the way!

Connor glanced up when, promptly at one o'clock, Dani reentered the office. He nodded briefly and returned to scheduling the rotation for next week's workload, trying to ignore her.

Not an easy task.

Connor was growing intrigued with the new secretary. He'd expected her to flounce around, ask a ton of questions, flirt with anything in jeans and play at office work.

So far the delicate-looking blonde had succeeded in getting an inspector out on a couple of hours' notice, had organized the mess of her desk and not flirted once. She ignored the men who stopped by with one excuse or another. Was she playing some game or was she for real?

He stared at her as she glanced through the phone messages he'd handed her earlier. After brushing back her blond mane, she picked up the phone and dialed the first number. She deliberately put a smile on her face, staring at the note in hand.

He frowned. What was she doing? Following up on problems was nothing to smile about.

And were those curls and waves natural? Must be. With the impatient way she brushed them out of her way, it was unlikely they were a perm gone wrong.

*Blonde* covered a variety of hues. Her hair was a mixture of gold, wheat-white and honey tumbling across her shoulders. Maybe she should have cut it like Catherine's, short and sleek. Or would those curls persist? Did they feel as soft and silky as they looked? Would they wrap around a man's fingers if he threaded his hands through them?

He glanced away. What was he doing, speculating about a woman's hair?

He rose and slammed out of the office, disgust warring with frustration. He'd told Mick that having a woman secretary was a bad idea.

Before he could decide whether to head for home to grab a bite to eat, check out what Mick was up to, or make sure Moose wasn't hotdogging with the crane, Connor spotted the county car descending the sweep of road leading to the site.

Taking a deep breath, he forced his mind on the upcoming inspection. He refused to think about Dani Winthrop and her wild mop of curls. Or her blue eyes. Or her sunny smile.

She'd be gone by Friday.

Connor didn't return to the office during the afternoon. Dani took advantage of his absence to question Mick. Getting a better picture of the operation would go a long way in bringing her up to speed. Plus the atmosphere in the office was much more relaxed, for which she was grateful.

There were phone calls to field, files to search for, and other routine tasks, in addition to trying to catch up with the work that had piled up since the former secretary had left.

But Dani persisted in asking questions as she tried to make sense of where they stood and how much they were trying to complete before closing down for winter.

By five she was glad to call it a day. It'd been hectic, but exhilarating work. And she was making progress. Now she would change into something comfortable and take a short walk before dinner. Another early night was on her schedule. She suspected it'd take a couple of days to get used to the hectic pace, in addition to the catch-up she needed to do.

Her doctor had told her to expect to grow tired more easily. How right she'd been.

Calling good-night to Mick, Dani headed for her trailer.

Two men lounged by the office steps when she descended.

"Evening, ma'am," one said.

She smiled and nodded, but kept walking.

They fell into step with her.

"Welcome to Windhaven's future newest resort," one said. "Or it will be when we're finished here. I'm Bill Frates. This here's Tim Harris."

"How do you do? I'm Dani Winthrop." She kept her pace brisk.

It was nice of them to introduce themselves, but she wasn't planning to become a good buddy to anyone. She'd do her job and keep to herself.

"It gets lonely eating dinner by yourself," Bill said. "Want to join us tonight?"

Dani increased her pace just a bit. "Thanks for the offer, but I have plans."

Only a few more yards to her trailer and safety. She resisted looking around to see if Connor was watching her. He'd surely consider this distracting his men.

"Tomorrow night then?"

"I'll have to see." She reached for her key and unlocked her door.

"It was nice meeting you both," she said politely.

Stepping inside, she closed the door and leaned against it for a moment. That was not distracting the men, as Connor had direly foretold. But it might come close. Too bad they didn't know she had no plans to get involved with anyone—even on a superficial level.

Marc's cruel defection had cured her of romantic notions. Some people were destined for happy ever after. She wasn't one of them.

She'd finally learned that lesson. She knew she had nothing to offer a man. Or was it men wanted something she couldn't provide? Her own father had run out on her mother before she'd been born. She'd never been serious with anyone be fore Marc. And he turned away once he heard about the baby. He'd found her fun to date for a while, but commitment hadn't been in his plans. Not to the baby and especially not to her.

She patted her tummy. "Whoever you are, sweetie, I'll love you forever," she whispered, an overwhelming glow of love swelling. She would cherish her child and never abandon it, no matter what the hardships.

As the baby grew and developed, so did her love for her unborn child. Dani wondered how her mother could have carelessly left her own daughter in foster care. Had she ever regretted forsaking her only child? Dani had been five when her mother had dumped her with social services, claiming she was unable to manage anymore.

Dani had made up tales when she was younger—about how her mother really adored her, but because she had no money, had had to reluctantly give her up to foster care, temporarily.

Then, in true melodramatic fashion, she had died, leaving Dani to languish in the system until she turned eighteen.

Of course, once she was older, Dani had figured out it was more likely her mother just hadn't wanted to be bothered. That she had found it easier to deal with life unencumbered by an unwanted child.

The old sorrows surfaced again and Dani pushed them away. It was all ancient history.

Her child would have all the love and devotion from its mother she could give it. And she had enough for two—to make up for Marc's defection. She would not let history repeat itself!

Soon she would no longer be alone—she'd have her precious baby. They'd be a happy, close family of two.

Ten minutes later, Dani peeked out her door. She'd put on loose shorts, a cotton top and a light sweatshirt. It was growing cooler by the minute, with the sun already behind the western peaks. But once she began walking she'd warm up.

No one appeared to be paying any attention to her. She locked her door and glanced around. Down by the lake a group of men were laughing and talking. Closer to her trailer, she saw four or five men near one of the campers, leaning back in camp chairs, shooting the breeze.

Taking a deep breath, she stepped out briskly. She waved when they called greetings, but didn't stop as she passed the group near the camper. Walking briskly, she headed for the lake. If she skirted the group there, she could head to the right and walk along the shore for a while.

If felt great to be outside after a day cooped up in the office. The air was scented with pine and a hint of fresh lake water. The dirt beneath her feet was so dry it puffed in little clouds as she walked. Her shoes would be covered in red dust by the time she got back.

The group by the lake grew quieter as she drew near. Circling around them, she once again smiled and waved. One man looked as if he planned to join her, but hesitated. She refused to make eye contact and hoped it would indicate she was not interested in companionship.

Small waves rippled quietly against the narrow beach. In spring, when the snow melted she suspected the water rose to the tree line. But by late summer, the level had dropped, so there was plenty of room to walk on the compacted soil at the water's edge.

Striding quickly along, Dani smiled with delight. It was the perfect ending to the day. She'd make a habit of this.

The water lapped gently at the shore. Wind rustled softly in the pines. By walking briskly, she kept warm, though she did slip on her sweatshirt. Maybe jeans would have been more suitable.

Before she'd gone too far, however, she was breathing hard.

She couldn't be that out of shape—she'd been walking a couple of miles after work every day in Denver. And the elevation here wasn't that much higher, was it?

By the time Dani decided to turn back, she was feeling decidedly queasy. Spots danced before her eyes and she was gasping for breath. A sharp pain pierced her head. She slowed her pace—anxious now only to return to the trailer and lie down.

Eyeing a fallen log near the lake, she considered sitting to rest for a moment, but pushed on. The light was fading fast. She needed to return to the trailer.

Once again she saw the men gathered near the water when she rounded the bend. Several were fishing. The others were drinking and laughing, unwinding after a tough day.

She stumbled, reached out to catch herself before she could fall. Then everything went black.

"Hey, boss, come quick. We've got a problem!" Bill Frates stopped running as soon as he spotted Connor.

Connor frowned and rose from where he'd been sitting beside the lake. This had better be good. The men knew the unwritten rule: don't bother the boss at twilight.

"What's wrong?" He quickly covered the distance to Bill.

"It's the new secretary. She fell and's unconscious."

Connor picked up his pace. "How did she fall?" he asked.

A sudden stab of fear struck him. She was all right, wasn't she? There was nothing wrong with her baby, was there? They were a half hour or longer from Carson Creek. Did the town have a helicopter for emergency airlifts?

Bill turned and hurriedly led the way back along the lake.

"She was just walking. A bunch of us were by the lake—you know how Tim and Sonny love fishing. We were all hanging out. So when she came into view, we watched her. Then she just dropped like a rock."

Connor saw the crowd of men. He began to run.

The men parted so Connor could get to the center of the group. Tim knelt beside her, gently shaking her shoulder and calling her name.

There on the ground lay Connor's new secretary. Her blond hair spread around her like a nimbus, highlighting the rusty-brown color of the ground. Her legs were bent, her arms outstretched. Her eyes were closed and her chest rose and fell quickly.

Connor swallowed hard and stooped down.

"Dani?"

He shook her shoulder gently. He glanced around.

"Did she trip on something? Who saw her fall?"

"A lot of us, boss," Tom Harmon said. "We were all watching her walk along, speculating if she'd speak to us on her way back, when she seemed to stumble, then just crumpled up. She didn't hit hard. We didn't see any rocks around."

The ground was strewn with a thick carpet of pine needles, which would have softened the hard-packed earth.

Connor gently patted her cheek. "Dani, wake up."

Her breathing was rapid and her color pale. He didn't know what was wrong, but whatever it was, it was worse because she was pregnant.

Slipping his arms beneath her shoulders and knees, he rose, holding her against her chest.

"Someone find Mick and have him call for an ambulance," Connor said, heading toward the trailers.

She didn't weigh a thing. Was she too thin? Against one arm, he could feel the softness of the skin beneath her knees. Her head was nestled on his shoulder, her fragrance swirling around him.

Ignoring the tingling tendrils of awareness, Connor pushed through the group and began the ascent to the trailers.

She stirred and opened her eyes, blinking a couple of times as she tried to get oriented.

"What happened?" She looked up into Connor's face.

"You took a tumble. Knocked yourself out, I think," he replied.

She rubbed her forehead with one hand and struggled. "Put me down. I can walk."

"We'll wait for the paramedics to determine that."

"I don't need paramedics. I'm fine. Put me down."

"Mick's calling an ambulance. You'll be in Carson Creek in no time."

"I'm not going to Carson Creek. I'm fine!" She pushed against his shoulder. "Really, Connor, this is embarrassing. Please, put me down."

He stopped. The group of men trailing behind him stopped. Slowly he set her on her feet, keeping his arm around her shoulders, watching for any sign of weakness.

Dani drew a deep breath and clutched his free arm. "I do feel a bit wobbly, but that's all. If I can just sit down, I'll be fine. Really, no paramedics."

He glanced at one of the men and nodded toward the office. "Catch Mick, tell him to hold off on the ambulance for the time being."

"Forever," Dani muttered, glancing around.

Color rose in her face. "Good grief," she murmured softly, "is the entire crew here?"

"I don't know who's here and who's not. It doesn't matter. Let's get you to your trailer. Then I want some answers."

They walked slowly, silently, to her trailer. She clung to his arm, but walked without further assistance. Behind them, the men began to disperse, until only Connor and Dani walked up to her steps. She dug her key from her pocket and inserted it. She opened the door, and he followed her in before she could protest.

Twice now she'd interrupted his evening routine. Did she plan to make a habit of it? He scowled. He knew she'd be trouble.

"I'm fine. Thanks for the rescue," she said, sinking down on her sofa. She leaned back and closed her eyes, her hands resting protectively on her stomach.

How was it he seemed to take all the air from the room? He towered over her and she kept her eyes closed to establish a modicum of control over the situation.

"What happened?" His voice was grim.

"I don't know. I was taking a walk. Then the next thing I knew, you were carrying me up the hill." She opened her eyes and looked at him. "No small feat these days."

He rubbed the back of his neck. "You didn't trip on anything?"

"No, but I have a piercing headache. I had it before I blacked out. I don't think I hit my head on anything."

"Altitude sickness, maybe?"

"Shouldn't be. I walk all the time in Denver."

"Which is several thousand feet lower in elevation. It takes a while to get acclimated to the high country."

"Noted."

"You're a liability here, Dani Winthrop. Not only to the job, but to yourself. What if you'd been injured? How long would it take an ambulance to get here? You're risking your own safety and that of your baby. You'll have to leave. We'll pay you for the week."

She flew to her feet and glared at him, her hands clenching into fists on her hips. "Now just a minute here, Connor Norris. You can't fire me for falling on my own time. I'm not hurt. Thank you for your concern, but I was hired to work for your company, and if you fire me for some trumped-up, bogus reason I'll sue you up one side and down the other!"

"A cheap price to pay—at least I'll know you and your baby are safe. It's too dangerous here for someone in your condition. I don't want anyone hurt. If you won't think about yourself, at least consider your child!" He glared at her for a long moment, then spun around and left.

Dani slowly sank back onto the sofa, her knees weak as wet spaghetti. What had that been about? It almost sounded as if he cared about her safety. Or was it only to minimize any liability to his precious construction site?

# Chapter Five

"Connor, what's going on? Is she all right?" Mick hurried over from the office, his face creased with worry.

Connor nodded.

"She fell. I think she fainted. It's not uncommon in pregnant women. And we're at a higher elevation from Denver. I think she overextended herself. She claims she's fine, but she's history. Get rid of her, Mick. You hired her, you fire her. She's a danger to herself and that baby."

He strode off, angry with the woman for taking risks.

Angry that he even cared.

The ache that took hold wouldn't let go. Catherine had never taken risks. She'd been careful her entire life—especially so when pregnant with Sammy.

And in the end, it hadn't mattered. It hadn't been enough.

But to deliberately take a risk when a child was involved was unacceptable. He wouldn't be a party to it.

Mick knocked on the trailer door. Dani answered immediately.

"Hi, Mick, come in." Stepping back, she smiled wryly. "I guess you heard."

"I came to see if you're all right."

"Honestly, I don't know what happened. One minute I'm

walking along, the next—"

The next she knew she'd been swept into the strongest pair of arms she'd ever felt. Connor had carried her up the incline from the lake as if she'd weighed nothing.

She could still feel the strength of his arms, the muscles of his chest. She couldn't ever remember anyone so strong, anyone who handled her so gently.

The special male scent that radiated from his skin seemed to linger and cause all sorts of reactions, just as it had in the office earlier. The heat that had enveloped her when she realized he was carrying her made her act silly. Once in the safety of her trailer, she'd lashed out in retaliation—and made an idiot of herself in the process. He'd only been watching out for her safety. There was nothing personal in his concern; he probably felt that way with all his employees.

She swallowed and sat down again, knees definitely wobbly. Should she listen to his advice? Leave when she'd just arrived—without even proving how competent she was?

She couldn't do that. She had too much riding on this job.

"Guess I tried too much. Connor suggested I'm suffering from altitude sickness. Can I use the phone in the office to call my doctor? Just to check in?"

"I can take you to the hospital in Carson Creek," Mick said instantly.

"Maybe, but first I'll check in with my regular obstetrician. I've heard of pregnant women fainting—although it's never happened to me before. Maybe Connor's right and it's just a reaction to the higher altitude. Which means I'll have to take it easy until I get used to being at this elevation. But I need to get some exercise. I can't just sit at a desk all day."

"Are you sure you don't want me to run you into town to be

checked by a doctor?"

"Let me check in with mine first."

Mick escorted her to the office, which was miraculously empty. Thankfully, Dani sat behind her desk, glad she didn't have to face Connor again so soon. She dialed the phone and spoke to the answering service, leaving her number. Hanging up, she looked at Mick.

"They'll track the doctor down for me. I'll just wait here until she calls back. Don't let me keep you from anything. I'm feeling fine, truly. I'm not going to keel over. Even my headache is fading."

"I'll sit with you. Maybe Connor was right. Maybe this is too much to expect of a pregnant woman," Mick said thoughtfully.

"Don't you start! We'll find out what happened and see it doesn't happen again. I need this job, Mick. Please don't fire me."

She hated having to plead to keep her job, but she could understand how, after this, they were uncertain she could last.

He looked uneasy. "I don't know if this will work, Dani."

"It will."

She wished she felt as confident as she had the day before. Had she placed the doubt in Mick's mind? She needed his support. Without it she was history. And then what was she going to do, where would she go?

He settled in behind his desk, leaning back in his chair, his feet on the desk as they waited for the doctor's call.

"Are you going back to Denver when the baby comes, or are you originally from somewhere else?" he asked.

"I have no family and no ties to Denver."

Especially after Marc's final rejection.

"I might check out Carson Creek over the next few weeks

to see if I like it. I can settle anywhere. And won't you need secretarial help again in the spring?"

She'd kept in touch with only one of her foster parents, but they weren't close. She had two friends from the building department and one longtime friend from high school. They all had busy lives and wouldn't miss her as much as she'd miss them.

Maybe she could start over in Carson Creek. Find a niche for herself and her baby.

Having a job to look forward to in the spring would help pass the long winter months.

Mick smiled. "You thinking about coming back when we start up again?"

"Maybe."

"And the baby?"

She looked around the office. "I think a playpen would fit in here by my desk. How long will you take to finish the project?"

"End of next summer should do it, if we keep on schedule and the winter doesn't last forever. Sorry, Dani, girl, Connor would never allow a baby on the site. It's too dangerous."

"Not in the office."

"It'll never happen, Dani. I'd back him on that decision. In fact, I need to know you'll be safe now or I'll change my position on your staying."

"I'm fine." Frustration was building. She wished she'd never gone on that blasted walk!

The phone rang.

Ten minutes later Dani hung up, feeling hugely relieved.

"The doctor said it sounds like altitude sickness. I'm to take things easy and drink a lot of fluids. If anything else happens, then I'm to see a local doctor immediately. I was planning to set up an appointment anyway, so I'll do that first thing in the morning."

"You're sure?" Mick asked. "I don't want anything to happen to you."

She nodded, warmed by his concern.

Hadn't Connor also been concerned?

The warmth she felt around Connor had nothing to do with *concern*.

"I was excited to have someone competent come all the way out here, I guess I didn't think things through completely," Mick said slowly.

"Don't even start thinking that way. I'm competent and capable. I'm not sick. Today was an anomaly. I can do the work, Mick. I've burned my bridges behind me. If you fire me, where would I go?"

She prayed this tactic might work with softhearted Mick. It never would with hard-as-nails Connor.

"Anyway, I think Connor overreacted," she said.

"Understandable."

"Why?" Did Mick hold insight into his partner, something that would enable her to better understand the man? To better deal with him? Could Mick help her find a way to work around Connor's antagonism and be allowed to remain?

"His wife and child were killed a few years ago. It eats at him that he wasn't there to save them. He probably feels he can at least make sure your baby's properly taken care of. And face it, Dani, a construction site isn't the safest place in the world. I should have thought through the situation more before hiring you. But we need help as much as you need the job."

She was stunned by the information about Connor's family. How tragic! She tried to imagine a loss of that magnitude.

Protectively, her hands covered her stomach. The worst fear of any parent was to lose a child. And he'd lost both wife and child?

"How were they killed?"

"Random shooting at an elementary school. Catherine was a teacher there, and Sammy had just started kindergarten." Mick's voice was heavy with grief.

"Oh, Lord." Dani swallowed, unexpected compassion and sympathy for Connor suddenly blooming. No wonder he was such a hard man—he'd have to be to survive such a devastating loss. "How awful!"

She wanted to weep—for the loss, for the man who must have been so devastated, so angry to lose his family in such a senseless manner.

Mick looked out the window, toward the skeleton of the lodge.

"He's never been the same. He and Catherine grew up together. Don't think he ever dated anyone else. And they doted on their little boy." Mick shook his head sadly. "Tragic time."

He turned and looked at Dani. "That's one reason he drives himself now—to forget, I think. If work is all-consuming, there's no time for memories."

"How long ago did it happen?"

Her throat ached with unshed tears. Her heart went out to the man. His attitude could be excused, explained.

Maybe he felt genuine concern for her and her pregnancy.

"Three years ago this month. It happened over in Fort Collins. That's where I had my company. Connor was my foreman at the time. Afterward, he had us push for bigger jobs, remote sites, shorter time schedules. He became my partner. His ideas are great and we're doing better than ever—but I miss that town. I don't reckon Connor will ever go back. He hasn't seen his folks since the funeral. Or Catherine's parents. We all lived in Fort Collins."

"I am so sorry," Dani said. "What happened to the gunman?"

"He turned the gun on himself before the cops could stop him. Which makes it even harder, I think—no one around to blame. Come on, I'll walk you back to your trailer. You feeling up to it?"

"Yes."

But there was something she needed to get straight.

"But this fainting doesn't matter to my position here. I'm not traipsing around the construction site, so I'm not in danger. Please, talk to Connor. I'll promise to do whatever you ask."

Mick studied her for a moment, then nodded. "We'll see what he says come Friday. We're partners, Dani. And I set a lot of store by his thinking. If we can't bring him around by Friday, then I think I'll have to go along with his decision."

She nodded, her optimism slipping. She'd hoped to count on Mick to argue on her behalf.

"I understand." And she did. If the shoe had been on the other foot, would she want an employee who proved to be a liability?

"If you want to go for a walk tomorrow, tell me. I'll go with you," Mick said as he stopped by her door.

"Thanks. I appreciate that."

"But just a gentle ramble, no trying out for the Olympics."

Dani laughed. "I wasn't!"

He nodded and gave her a friendly pat on the shoulder. Dani let herself out of the office, relieved that her doctor had not seemed concerned. But fainting wasn't something she wanted to repeat.

Was there a certain wisdom in Connor's wanting her to leave?

After a hot shower and a quick meal, Dani sat on the sofa in her living area for a long time, her mind wandering to the revelations Mick had made, trying to assimilate the horror of the tragedy with Connor and his family. No wonder the man was as hard as nails. He'd have to be to survive such a loss.

It gave her a different view of her boss, maybe one she could figure out how to tap into. She not only had to prove she'd be a valuable member of the team, but also that she was in no danger. Today's fainting spell hadn't helped. Maybe she could have him talk directly to her doctor. Would that reassure him?

Wasn't anything ever easy she wondered with a sigh as she rose to wash her plate and utensils. It sure hadn't been so far.

The primrose-yellow dress Dani donned the next morning was soft and feminine. She stared at herself in the mirror, suddenly struck by her image. Maybe she was her own worst enemy. No wonder Connor doubted her abilities, her suitability at the construction site and her safety. She looked as if she were heading out for a tea party or something. Her own style in clothes was working against her.

Quickly she changed into a dark, hunter-green dress that seemed more businesslike, and tied her hair back, trying to look as competent as she could. There was only so much she could do with her hair. She frowned at her reflection, deciding she still looked too soft for a construction site.

She needed to go into town and get some jeans and flannel shirts. Her own jeans were in storage in Denver. Not that they'd fit, anyway, these days. Maybe she'd even get some boots. If she dressed like everyone else on the site, then maybe Connor wouldn't even notice she was different.

Saturday she'd make the trip to Carson Creek to see about expanding her wardrobe. Until then, she had only her skill and experience on the job going for her. It would have to do.

Neither Connor nor Mick were in the office when Dani entered. She gave a sigh of relief. She had plenty to do. They'd undoubtedly have more tasks when they returned.

She liked working alone. Otherwise, she was self-conscious with Connor staring at her, listening to her phone conversations, judging her with his critical attitude.

Or distracting her by just sitting in his chair!

She had completed the calls Connor had requested she handle and was once again plunged into matching invoices and purchase orders. There was a discrepancy with one vendor—Andrews Tool and Die. Curious, she pulled out the folder on the company. It was thick, showing years of a business relationship with the firm.

Further research turned up other discrepancies. The cost overruns and extra billings added up to a tidy sum over a period of several months.

Did Mick and Connor know this? She noted scrawled initials in the corners of the invoices. Obviously Pete had obtained approvals to pay. From whom?

When Connor entered the office some time later, Dani forgot about business, seeing only the man who had lost his family so tragically.

She immediately wanted to extend her sympathies, but one glance at his dark expression, and she wisely kept her mouth shut.

In fact, she suddenly wondered how he'd react if he

discovered Mick had been talking about him. Today was Thursday, not an auspicious time to take a chance. She had only today and tomorrow to prove herself. Making him angry wouldn't be a smart move.

She reached for the phone when it rang. It was her doctor checking on her again. She spoke briefly, and when she hung up, Connor was studying her.

"My doctor. I talked with her last night and she wanted to see how I was doing today. I'm fine. She said to just take it slow adjusting to the higher altitude. Which won't be a problem. I know what to look for now and it won't happen again!"

He gave nothing away in those dark eyes, just nodded once and returned to the site drawing he was marking.

When the phone rang again, Dani snatched it up, grateful for the interruption. Would anything change his mind?

"Mr. Stephenson calling for Mr. Norris," a smooth voice on the other end said.

Dani held up the phone. "A Mr. Stephenson for you."

Connor took the call.

Dani half listened to the one-sided conversation. It was hard to get the gist from his yes and no and that-would-be-fine comments. When he hung up, he glanced over at her.

"Stephenson is the liaison between our firm and Windhaven's board. He'll be out next week to check on our progress."

She nodded, a small bud of hope blossoming. Was Connor telling her because she'd be here next week and needed to know? He must be, otherwise why bother clarifying the situation?

He turned back to the clipboard he'd brought into the office and jotted some notes on a sheet of paper.

Dani watched him, wondering how he'd felt when first

informed of his son's death. Of the wanton killing of his wife—especially when he'd loved her since they were kids.

Dani wondered what it would be like to be loved like that. To know someone from when she'd been little and still have a deep relationship.

He looked up and caught her eye. "Something wrong?"

She shook her head. "Did you need me to do something special for Mr. Stephenson's visit?"

She was glad he couldn't read minds. But she wished she could.

Connor rocked back in his chair, balancing it on two legs as he scanned the office, apparently lost in thought. A moment later, he looked at her and brought his chair back on all four legs.

"You're an adult. Mick convinced me last night that if you think you can be safe here, I have to grant that you can run your own life. Your work has been exemplary. But it's still early. I'm willing to give you another week's trial."

Dani nodded, hiding the sudden glee that swept through her. Thank goodness for Mick. Obviously his opinion counted a lot in this partnership.

"Do you suppose you could get this place cleaned up by Monday afternoon? Stephenson and his team will want to go over things and we could do it here if the place looked halfway decent."

Dani vowed right then and there to have the office spotless by the time Monday rolled around. She planned to make herself indispensable. Here was another way to prove it to Connor.

Another week. How much more could she prove her worth in another week? She kept her expression pleasant, trying desperately to hide the joy that flooded her. She could do it.

And maybe get a chance to see the man smile!

She blinked, wondering where that thought had come from. She didn't care if he ever smiled as long as she stayed employed.

She resumed her review of the invoices from Andrews Tool and Die with renewed fervor. Jotting notes on a separate sheet, she realized that each invoice had billed a minor amount beyond what it should have. But when she tallied everything for the last two years, it came to a total that was staggering.

Mick entered the office, tossed his hard hat on his desk and headed for the pot of coffee.

"That wind's cold today. Hope it's not the leading edge of a storm."

"Nothing forecast for the next week. Don't borrow trouble. I heard from Paul Stephenson. He'll be here on Monday." Connor looked up at Mick, then nodded toward Dani.

"She said she could get the place decent by then. One of their publicists and an accountant are coming, too."

Mick looked suspiciously at Connor then at Dani.

She smiled at Mick, wishing she could thank him for talking to Connor after he'd seen her home last night. Later for sure, but not in front of Connor.

"Oh, well, good. Guess she's staying, then." Mick winked at her.

"For another week's trial," Connor said.

He couldn't dim her delight in the extension Dani thought defiantly. She'd become indispensable in a week. Watch out, Connor!

The morning passed swiftly after that. Just before lunch, Dani put down her pencil and looked at the two men. She was sure of her facts, but wasn't sure how they'd react.

"I think I've found a problem," she said slowly.

Both men looked up at her.

"It appears that one of your vendors has been siphoning off a bit more with each invoice than you have on your purchase orders."

"What vendor?" Connor asked, glancing at Mick.

"Andrews Tool and Die."

"What!" he said, rising to storm over to her desk. "Let me see that!"

"Oh, Lord!" Mick said, sitting at his desk, his latest cup of coffee held precariously as he looked at her in dismay.

Dani didn't know what she'd just done, but by the dark scowl on Connor's face it had to be terrible. Was this what would get her fired?

# Chapter Six

"Let me see that," Connor repeated, holding out his hand for the folder and sheets of paper.

She held on to the folder. "I've been catching up—matching the invoices and purchase orders with the check register you send to the accountant. This batch is three months behind. I couldn't help noticing discrepancies with this account."

"It'll be taken care of," Connor said curtly. He wiggled his fingers impatiently and Dani reluctantly placed the folder in his hand.

He spun around and glared at Mick. "Not a word," he warned.

Mick shrugged and went back to his blueprint.

Dani didn't understand. "Did you already know about it?" she asked.

Connor dropped the file on his desk and sat down, his familiar scowl present.

"I'll take care of the matter. Why don't you take off for lunch? It's almost twelve."

Recognizing that she'd been clearly dismissed, Dani nodded and rose. She walked carefully from the office and turned just before she closed the door behind her. Connor was staring at the closed folder. She couldn't describe the expression on his face, but if she had to make a guess, she'd call it bleak.

"What was that all about?" she wondered aloud as she crossed the sunny clearing.

Neither man had displayed the reaction she'd expected.

The wind was stronger than before, and carried the hint of fall in it, cool and biting. Walking briskly, she was glad to reach the shelter of her trailer. Maybe this would be all the walking she did today.

A couple of the men called a greeting. She smiled and waved. So far only Bill and Tim had introduced themselves. Though given the chance, she suspected some who wandered into the office would have, except that Connor or Mick had always been present.

Dani put her feet up while she ate, relishing the brief respite in the busy day. She wondered if she'd have more energy if she upped her vitamin intake.

When the knock at the door came several moments later, it startled her. Not one of the workers, surely.

She opened it. Connor stood at the foot of the steps. "I want to speak with you—privately," he said.

Oh great, was he going to fire her? Just for doing her job? Or was that the excuse he'd use?

"Come in."

She stepped aside to let him in, aware again of how much he seemed to fill the small space of her living room. She wondered how he felt in his own trailer—cramped? Or was it larger than hers, offering more space?

He looked around, noticing the chair pulled up in front of the sofa, the plate with her half-eaten sandwich set to one side.

"Resting?" he asked.

"Just putting my feet up for a little while. Is this a short visit or would you like to sit down?"

He turned and looked at her, a hint of amusement dancing in his eyes. It was as unexpected as it was intriguing.

Dani stared at him. It made him look approachable, almost human. Again she wondered what he'd look like if he ever smiled.

"You fascinate me, Dani Winthrop," he said. "Most people in your position would be fawning over me, doing all they could to curry favor so I'll let them stay. As a welcome, your invitation lacks hospitality."

"If my work won't speak for me, fawning over you isn't going to help matters," she said shortly, flustered by the intensity of his gaze. His eyes were so dark as to be almost black. She could stare into them for hours.

"My visit won't take long, but sit back down. I don't want you interrupting your rest time." Connor pulled one of the dining chairs from the nearby table and turned it, straddling it and resting his arms on the back. He waited until she resumed her seat on the sofa before speaking again.

"Mick and I had a rather heated discussion after you left," he began.

"About?"

She knew what about—her staying. What else?

"About the Andrews Tool and Die discrepancies you found and the need-to-know principle."

"Need-to-know principle?"

"You know, what do you need to know to do your job, and what is just–idle gossip."

"I don't have a clue what you are talking about. I thought you came to fire me."

"Next week's not up yet. And I'm not inclined to fire

someone for doing a good job. Mick convinced me you need to know what's going on to better do your job, and not go off half-cocked on some tangent that's already been dealt with."

Dani nodded, hoping her total confusion didn't show.

"Don't you want to put your feet up? You only have a few minutes left for lunch break," he said.

Self-consciously, she lifted her feet to the chair, glad for the full skirt that covered most of her legs. He watched her every move. It flustered her. Why had he come? What couldn't have waited until she returned to the office?

"So my need to know?" she prompted.

"We fired Pete, right before he was arrested for embezzling funds. By the same method you uncovered today—approving padded invoices, splitting the difference with greedy clerks at the various vendors. He always did the reconciliation, so we didn't catch on right away. But we haven't advertised the fact of his arrest. I doubt any of the men here know. Mick and I want to keep it that way."

"He was arrested?" It was the last thing she'd expected to hear.

Connor nodded. "We've kept it as quiet as possible—so as not to spook investors, and to enable law enforcement officials to find and deal with those involved at the various vendors who participated in his scheme."

"And Andrews Tool and Die is another company involved—but one you didn't know about before," she guessed.

Connor sighed, tightening his jaw. "Right. We never suspected it."

He studied her for a moment, then continued, "Marshal Andrews is my brother-in-law."

"Uh-oh," she said softly.

Connor gave a mirthless laugh. "Uh-oh doesn't begin to describe it. I want to handle this one differently. Mick doesn't agree, but said he'll hold off notifying the authorities until Monday."

Dani nodded. "I won't tell a soul."

"Discreet as well as competent," he murmured. He hesitated a moment, then added, "You could use this as a bargaining tool."

"For what?" she asked.

"For keeping your job. Your silence in exchange for continued employment."

Dani's temper flared up. Honestly, the man was enough to drive her crazy! She didn't remember getting so angry so often in her entire life before this week. Down came her feet, and she surged up from the sofa.

"That's despicable. I would never do such a thing! How dare you even suggest it!"

Standing, she was taller than Connor. He gazed up at her, almost mesmerized by her appearance. Color stained her cheeks, the rosy hue deepening the blue of her eyes, which flashed with fire and anger. Even tied back as it was, her hair seemed to shimmer around her like a glowing halo trembling with indignant rage.

Her lips were tight with disapproval. But Connor knew what they looked like softened, smiling. For a moment he was struck with wondering what they'd feel like. Warm and supple? Sweet and feminine?

He scowled and rose to his own feet, putting distance between them. He had no business thinking about kissing Dani Winthrop! He'd sworn off even the thought of getting interested in another woman after Catherine died. Even thinking about kissing someone else seemed a betrayal of his love for his wife.

But it had been three long years and his body was betraying him with its reaction to this petite, feminine fireball.

"I said that you could have used this, not that you would. I don't want this to get out. Mick and I will handle it and turn it over to the proper authorities if warranted. But I want to talk to Marshal first."

The fact was he didn't want to believe his brother-in-law would stoop to crime. He hoped for some explanation. For Catherine's sake, he'd investigate on his own before turning any information over to the authorities.

"Fine." Dani continued to glare at him.

"I'll be heading back to the office."

He'd gotten her compliance, but at a cost. She looked mad enough to spit!

She didn't say a word.

"Take some extra time if you need it," he said, backing toward the door, unable to take his eyes from her. Could he add something to calm the tension? Or was retreat the best plan?

"I'll be there at one," she snapped.

"Good, good."

Connor opened the door and stepped outside as quickly as he could, closing it behind him. Retreat was definitely called for. He needed his own space, away from those flashing eyes, those bewitching blond curls. She could have him forgetting his own name if she half tried.

Which, in all honesty, he had to admit she never had. Maybe she was too good to be true. She had done nothing except do the work for which she'd been hired. No tricks, no flirting, no promising anything she hadn't delivered.

Striding quickly toward the office, he changed his mind

halfway there and headed for the lake. Connor wasn't ready to return to the tasks at hand, and certainly not ready to confront Marshal Andrews with the information Dani had turned up.

Men drifted past, nodding, calling a greeting, heading back to the job site. Connor barely acknowledged the greetings, lost in thought as he was.

He had to come to terms with his growing awareness of Dani Winthrop before he could do anything else.

Not awareness—not on a sexual level. That was too strong.

Interest?

No, not that.

She was an employee only. Nothing more.

But the memory of her sparkling eyes seemed to tease him, the curiosity about how her hair would feel continued to plague him until he could hardly keep his hands to himself. And her anger only made his fascination grow stronger.

Maybe it was the glow pregnant women had.

Like she'd be a hag when she wasn't pregnant? Hardly.

He wasn't ready to deal with this. Maybe he never would be. It was time to focus on the job and keep his distance from Dani Winthrop and the disturbing thoughts that plagued him whenever he looked at her.

# Chapter Seven

On Saturday morning Dani slept in until nine. She reveled in knowing she had two days totally to herself. Not that she planned to spend the weekend in complete relaxation. There was more to do in the office in order to have it spotless for the meeting on Monday. But she had definitely made progress.

Thanks to Connor's staying away since lunch on Thursday.

She'd been angry when she returned to the office, only to find he was busy on the site. By Friday afternoon, when he still hadn't put in an appearance in the office, she began to wonder if he were deliberately avoiding the place. But why?

She'd have thought it was because of their discussion at lunch on Thursday, but Connor definitely was not the type to let a small confrontation like that deter him from anything he wanted to do. He'd just charge onward.

After a leisurely breakfast, she headed into Carson Creek. She had shopping to do—both for clothes and groceries. And she wanted to explore the town and see what it was like.

Wearing the bright yellow dress she'd discarded a couple of days earlier, she decided she was still determined to buy jeans and shirts. Once that was accomplished, Dani planned to treat herself to lunch and wander around, sightseeing a little before getting her groceries. She'd brought her cooler to carry the perishables, and she planned to stock up this trip, convinced she'd stay the course.

Some time later, she stowed the many packages of new clothes in the trunk of her car and turned to survey the main street of the small mountain town. She'd been lucky to find a clothing store that had a couple of pairs of maternity jeans that fit her, with waistbands that would expand as she did. The flannel shirts felt warm and cozy. She was into comfort more and more these days.

The boots were instantly comfortable. Maybe she should have worn her new jeans and boots and carried the dress home, she mused. But it was too late now; everything was stashed in the car.

Main Street was lined with parked cars and trucks. The old buildings were mostly wood, with a brick one here and there, and a faded brown stucco building at the far end of town. The false fronts were common in towns in Colorado, but she enjoyed looking at them nonetheless.

She walked down the street, peering into wide shop windows, enjoying the different displays of books, yarn and fabrics, hardware, wood-burning stoves and colorful liquor bottles.

Finally she reached the diner.

Glancing in through the windows, she stopped, reconsidering. It seemed full—mostly of men. There were five at the counter, and almost every table was occupied. She recognized a couple of men from the work site. The rest were strangers. Two women were eating at one table, but there didn't appear to be a single woman on her own.

And none dressed as she was. She should have worn her new jeans.

"Coming or going?" a familiar voice asked.

Dani spun around to see Connor standing beside her. She glanced behind him. No Mick.

Trying to ignore the fluttering in her tummy, she smiled brightly. "I was going in to eat, but it seems crowded."

She didn't want him to know she felt intimidated.

"There're a couple of tables vacant," he said, looking over her head into the diner.

"Oh." She glanced back through the window, stalling.

What was he doing here? If he'd leave, she could find another place to eat where she wouldn't stick out like a sore thumb.

"Are you in town shopping?" she asked, turning back to look at him.

"I'm here to pick up a few things, order more. We have a small order ready at the hardware store. Right now I want lunch."

"Oh."

He studied her for a moment, then sighed. "Care to join me?"

Eat with Connor? Have to sit across the table from him and talk with him for up to an hour? Her heart was already beating as fast as if she'd run a race. Her stomach felt full of butterflies. Could she eat a thing with him sitting that close? What would they talk about?

He inclined his head slightly. Aware of the seconds ticking by, Dani nodded and took a deep breath.

"That would be nice," she said politely, hunger winning the internal debate.

When they entered, the people seated near the door glanced up, but no one seemed to pay them special attention. She wound her way through the crowded area to a vacant table near the rear and sat down gratefully, looking around curiously.

The diner had linoleum flooring and chrome-edged tables and chairs. The decor seemed straight from the 1950s. The heavenly aroma that filled the air had her mouth watering even before the waitress dropped two menus on the table and placed two brimming glasses of water before them.

"I'll give you a couple of minutes," she said, and walked away.

Marc would never have eaten in a place like this, Dani thought, picking up the menu. He was into show and flash. And being seen. This place looked as if it served good hearty food to one and all, for inexpensive prices. No linen tablecloths, no cloth napkins.

But she liked it. It had charm.

Carefully keeping her gaze on her menu, Dani desperately sought a topic of conversation she could safely discuss with Connor. They had nothing in common. And there was a certain amount of antagonism on his part. He wanted her gone.

Maybe she could ask him about Monday's meeting or about the future plans of the resort or—

"Ready to order?" he asked.

Dani peeped over the menu and found his dark gaze fixed on her. She swallowed hard, hoping he couldn't guess how flustered she felt.

Nodding quickly, she looked for the waitress. Connor signaled and the woman hurried over.

Marc would be envious of Connor's air of command. He never received such swift attention, Dani thought, childishly pleased in a perverse way. Much as she told herself she was over the man, the lingering hurt never quite went away.

After they ordered, she took a breath and prepared to start the conversation, but Connor startled her by asking bluntly, "Where's your baby's father?"

She blinked. She hadn't expected that. "He lives in Denver," she said.

"And?"

"And what?"

"Why is he there and you here? A falling out?"

"You could say that. He doesn't want to be a father."

Connor looked away, a brief expression of pain crossing his face before he schooled it to impassivity.

Dani remembered that his own son had been killed by a crazed gunman. Obviously Connor was still grieving. He was a father who had wanted his child. Why couldn't her baby's father want it?

"Not all men want babies, I guess," she said.

"Then he's a fool. Being a father is the most incredible experience in the world."

"I'm sorry for the loss of your son and your wife." There, she'd said it. She'd wanted to ever since Mick had mentioned it.

Connor narrowed his eyes as he looked back at her. "Mick told you?"

She nodded. "I can't even imagine how awful it must have been."

"Still is," he said shortly. "It's not something I talk about. And Mick has no business gossiping about me behind my back."

"It wasn't gossip. I think he was trying to let me know why you reacted so strongly when I fainted the other day."

She turned her water glass, watching the ice bob gently on the surface.

"I've heard it's the worst thing, a parent losing a child. I can't imagine losing my baby. Or giving it up." She said the words so softly she didn't think he'd hear.

But he had.

"Did the father want you to give it up?"

"No. Actually, he wanted me to have an abortion. I refused, and that was the end of his involvement in my life. A child didn't fit in with his image of the perfect life. I didn't, either."

Not in the perfect, shallow existence Marc enjoyed.

"Are you thinking of giving the baby up for adoption?"

"No! I would never do such a thing." Dani looked directly into his eyes. "I already love this baby. I'll do anything to keep it."

"Some people, especially single women, give their kids up for adoption. It's not necessarily a bad thing."

"Well, I'm not some people. I can afford to take care of a child and I will, no matter how tough the going gets. Businesses always need good secretaries and I am good."

"Modest, too."

She grinned. "If you've got it, flaunt it!"

"Planning to return to Denver?"

Dani thought about it a moment. "Probably not. I have nothing to tie me there. I can really go anywhere. I might look for an apartment or small house to rent here in Carson Creek." She looked at him. "Then I'd be handy in the spring when construction starts up again."

Connor looked startled. "You haven't even worked through next week and you're planning to be back next spring? It'll never happen."

"We'll see."

She wished he'd stop staring at her. She'd never be able to eat if her stomach didn't settle down. Or if she didn't stop feeling she was about to hyperventilate. His steady gaze made her very nervous, and very conscious that he was all male.

For the first time in more than four months, she was aware of a man. Aware and growing interested.

That would never do. She must remember her vow—no more involvement except on a superficial level. There was too much heartache in growing attached to people. They always left in the end.

"Maybe I'll find a job here in town. It seems like a nice place to raise a child. If I do a great job for you, you would write me a recommendation, wouldn't you?"

Connor nodded, suddenly aware he didn't like thinking of her going elsewhere. Not that he wanted her to work at the site next spring. What would she do with the baby during the day?

Next spring?

What had happened to his thinking that she wouldn't last the week?

In only a few days, he'd grown used to her bright smile and unflagging optimism and energy. It was a refreshing change from Mick's lackadaisical attitude. Or the doomsayers from Windhaven's accounting office.

Connor had stayed away from Dani as much as he could the last couple of days, but it hadn't blotted her from his mind.

Even his quiet evening at the lake last night had been spoiled as he subconsciously waited for her to show up needing him for some crisis.

He didn't like where his thoughts were going. Hoping to shake things up, he leaned back in his chair and said,

"No wonder you wanted to come to a construction site— plenty of men to choose from to take care of you and that baby."

He could have predicted her reaction. Heck, he had counted on it.

Raging color flooded her cheeks, and her blue eyes deepened and flashed fire. He could swear her hair almost stood on end.

He had to give her credit, however. She didn't cause a scene, didn't dump ice water in his lap or storm out of the diner. She leaned forward, her teeth gritted.

"That's the most asinine thing I've heard in ages. You are one dumb chauvinistic male if you think women want a man in their life to take care of them. This is the twenty-first century, and I can take care of myself!"

"So you don't want a man?"

"No!"

He tilted his head slightly. She appeared to be telling the truth. But a woman alone with a baby? It had been hard enough when he and Catherine shared duties with Sammy. How did single parents manage?

"Still pining for the baby's father?"

Dani drew herself up in the chair and glared at him. "Not that it is any of your business, but no. Once he showed his true colors, I knew he was not the man for me. Had never been, in fact, but I had been blinded by his apparent interest and flattered by his attention. Heady stuff to someone who had never had it."

"Never had what?"

She glanced away, looked at her glass, finally darted a quick look at Connor.

"Love," she mumbled.

"First boyfriend?"

He found that hard to believe. With that cascading blonde hair, those bright eyes and her frequent smile, she probably stepped on men's hearts like some women climbed stairs.

"This is embarrassing. I don't want to discuss it."

"It isn't a discussion. Just answer the question."

"Marc was not my first boyfriend, but he was the first one I thought might stick around."

"So your mama didn't warn you about men who liked to, er, play the field?"

"My mother abandoned me when I was five. I never saw her again. My dad split before I was born."

Connor stared at her, dumbfounded. The color in her cheeks was fading. Her eyes looked everywhere but at him.

*She had been abandoned as a child?*

How could any parent abandon his or her own child?

The old familiar ache began. He'd give his right arm to have another minute with Sammy. Or Catherine. He had spent as much time with them as he'd been able and it hadn't been enough. How could someone just throw that away?

"What happened with your mother?" he asked, unable to imagine anyone giving up a child.

"I have no idea. I said I never saw her again. She dumped me at social services one day, told them she couldn't afford to feed me, and left before they could stop her."

"And she never contacted you again?"

Dani shook her head. "I went into foster care. Lived with a couple of nice families—but it's not the same as blood kin."

"People don't have to be blood related to be a family," he said.

She shrugged. "It seemed like that to me growing up."

He was silent, trying to come to terms with her revelation. If he'd been abandoned by his parents, would he have such a sunny disposition? Heck, he'd been raised by doting parents and didn't have a sunny disposition.

The waitress made her way among the tables, balancing their plates on her arm. She set the plates in front of them and asked to make sure they had everything they wanted, and sashayed away.

Connor didn't notice. He was still trying to figure out a way to respond to Dani's revelation. Had she tried to find her parents? She must have been an adorable little girl, since she was pretty enough to penetrate his own hard shell. How could—

"Do you come here every Saturday?" she asked brightly, obviously changing the subject.

He didn't want to change it. He wanted to know more. But he followed her lead.

It wasn't the end of their discussion, however. She just didn't know it yet.

"Every once in a while I go to Durango or up to Grand Junction. Depends if I can combine business with weekend travel. But usually Carson Creek's as good as it gets. The food here isn't bad."

"No, it's delicious. I wasn't sure if it was just because I hadn't fixed it."

Silence stretched out between Dani and Connor. The soft murmur of the other diners provided background noise.

Connor didn't feel the need to say much. He'd already put his foot into it a couple of times. No sense in making matters worse.

But he didn't like the silence.

"Have you seen the town?" he asked at last.

"I was in the grocery store last Tuesday, and plan to go there after lunch to stock up for the week. And today I bought some more clothes—warmer things for the fall. I thought I'd walk around before I leave. Some of the houses on the side streets look intriguing."

"They were probably built during the gold boom, which didn't last long here. Cripple Creek drew the miners. I find Victorian architecture enduring."

"And pretty. I'm glad so many owners have been able to maintain the homes."

You couldn't get much more superficial than that, Connor thought cynically. Maybe he should introduce the weather as the next topic.

When they finished, Dani brought out her wallet and carefully counted out several dollars. She dropped some beside her place and held out the rest.

"Dutch, of course," she said firmly.

"We could talk about work for a minute or two and write it off," he suggested whimsically.

He wouldn't pad an expense account, but she needn't know that if it would save face. It didn't set right, her paying for her lunch. He suspected every bit she saved now would help when the baby came.

Not that her preparation—or lack—was any of his business.

"I'll pay my own way," she said firmly.

The lunch crowd had thinned. They quickly paid and walked out into the afternoon sunshine.

"It's so nice in the sun, but actually quite cool in the shade," she said, tilting her face to the sunshine.

Connor felt a kick in his gut. He wanted to kiss her, see if the sun-warmed skin tasted as sweet and warm as it looked.

"Oh!" Her eyes flew open and her hand went to her stomach. "Goodness, what a kick. Is he doing somersaults?" She looked at Connor shyly. "Would you like to feel?" she asked hesitantly.

No!

The memories of Sammy were too poignant. How often had he and Catherine marveled over the feel of that little person inside her? How often had they shared the intimacies of the baby they'd created growing in his mother?

Dani didn't wait for an answer, but took Connor's hand and placed it on the small mound of her stomach.

Connor felt it, definitely a firm kick. Or elbow.

Memories flooded back. The aching pain threatened to overwhelm him. Before he could pull away, however, Dani smiled up to him, pure happiness shining in her eyes.

"I've never been able to share that with anyone before. Isn't it great?"

He left his hand in place, sharing the wondrous miracle of life for as long as he could bear it.

Time and place blurred. He looked at Dani and saw Catherine. But not the strong image he was used to. She seemed fuzzy and Dani came into sharp focus.

Leaning over, he brushed back the soft curls, tucking them behind her ear, relishing the satiny feel of the tresses he'd so longed to touch.

"Cherish your baby, Dani. Hold on to every precious moment."

Without another word, Connor turned and strode off, the anguish of his loss threatening to overwhelm him.

# Chapter Eight

Dani stared after the man, stunned by his gentle touch. She raised her hand to her cheek, still feeling the warmth of his fingertips where he'd brushed back her hair. Still feeling the thrill of his palm against her belly, where her baby continued to do the cancan.

She wasn't touched often and usually in the most impersonal manner—a stranger brushing against her in a crowded street, or a friendly handshake when meeting someone.

This was outside her realm. Her skin felt sensitized and exceptionally responsive. Her nerve endings tingled and a vague yearning for something beyond her experience rose.

Connor was a puzzling man. Harsh and abrupt, opinionated and decisive, yet obviously capable of gentleness and perception.

*Cherish your baby, Dani. Hold on to every precious moment.*

The words echoed in her mind. She felt a sharp ache at his loss. How did he make it through each day, knowing his own baby was dead, their precious moments together gone forever?

She should cut him some slack. Had he changed when he lost so much? What would it take to ease some of that pain?

He seemed to be a man who had cared deeply, unlike Marc, who was content to live in the moment—as long as the moment centered around him. How could she have not seen that at the time?

She was on her guard now. Not trusting her own judgment, not certain she could ever trust it, she vowed to stay away from entangling relationships, no matter how tantalizing it might be to fantasize about a man adoring her, caring for her, sharing her life.

She and her baby would be enough.

With that thought firmly locked in place, she turned in the opposite direction and started out to explore Carson Creek.

By mid afternoon, she'd tired of wandering through the quaint mountain town. She wanted to buy her groceries and get back before dark. She might take a short stroll to the lake's edge before dinner, if she had the time and inclination, but she really had had enough walking for now.

Dani pulled into the parking slot next to her temporary home some time later. Mick stuck his head out of a window in his trailer as she climbed from the car.

"I'll be right there to help you carry things inside," he called.

"I can manage," she said with a wave.

But he obviously didn't listen well. In two minutes he was pushing open her door, a sack of groceries in each arm.

"You shouldn't be carrying all these heavy bags. Tell the bag boy to put fewer items in each one. Makes for more bags, but if I'm not around, you won't have to strain to lift them."

Dani hid a smile and nodded gravely. The bags weren't that heavy. She knew her limitations and wouldn't exceed them.

"Want to go for a walk later on?" Mick asked, when all the food had been put away, and the bags of new clothes placed on her bed.

"I think I've had enough walking today, I wandered all over Carson Creek."

"How about tomorrow, then?" he said.

"Maybe in the afternoon. I want to finish up in the office in preparation for Monday's meeting first. Shall we make it a picnic? We could walk along the lake for a while until we find a sunny place to eat."

As long as the weather held, Dani thought she should take advantage of the location and explore all she could. She loved the quiet of the woods when the heavy equipment wasn't operating. The pristine beauty of the lake soothed her whenever she gazed at it.

"That sounds fine, Dani girl. I'll be here around noon."

"What time will the Windhaven people arrive on Monday, do you know?"

"Not until afternoon, I expect. They usually fly into Grand Junction, drive to Carson Creek and then out here. I bet they'll eat lunch in Carson Creek. That's what they did last visit."

"That gives us more time to get ready, though I don't think we'll need it. I thought they'd be here first thing," Dani said as she finished putting up the last of the canned goods.

"Naw, Paul Stephenson likes his comforts. Once we have a few rooms completed in the resort, I'm sure he'll stay here. But until then, he spends as little time here as he can. Carson Creek isn't up to his standards, but it beats roughing it in a trailer."

Dani was reminded of Marc and his love for expensive restaurants and first-class accommodations. Paul Stephenson sounded like that. Why did men like that get into jobs where they had to rough it?

Her thoughts veered toward Connor. He didn't seem to mind roughing it. He fit right in with the rough-and-tumble site, the rugged, rustic camp. A man's man.

Yet he'd proved today he had a tender side.

Her heart skipped a beat. She had to stop thinking about him, about their lunch and the sweet way he'd brushed back her hair before he'd left so abruptly.

"Do they come often?" she asked, trying to focus on anything but Connor.

"Every couple of months, so far. I expect this to be the last visit until we start up again in the spring. What can I bring for the picnic?" Mick asked.

"Not a thing. I'll pack some sandwiches and drinks. There's a big blanket in the closet that will be perfect. You can carry everything."

"Done. See you then."

Mick patted her on the shoulder as he left.

Dani felt a special warmth toward the older man, unlike the fluttering feelings she experienced around Connor. If she was up to another risk, she might wish to get to know Mick better.

Was he lonely, living so far from his home, knowing he probably wouldn't go back to Fort Collins anytime soon? At least not as long as he followed his footloose partner.

Turning, Dani wandered back into her postage-stamp-size kitchen. Maybe she'd bake something for their picnic. It would give her a chance to be creative. And hopefully take her mind off Connor. The incident at lunch replayed over and over in her mind. She needed to do something to dislodge that!

Early Sunday morning, Dani headed for the office to prepare for Monday's meeting. She dusted all the desks and chairs and bookcases, straightening the piles of paper on the partners' desks.

Looking around the office some time later, she smiled in

pride. The office looked professional and a whole sight better than the first day she'd seen it.

It was a bit cramped with the makeshift conference table in the center, but with everything put away, it would do.

Time to get ready for her picnic.

She donned loose denim shorts and sturdy walking shoes for her outing with Mick. Her pink cotton top was loose, the color flattering. Her stomach still didn't stretch it to its limits. She would need maternity tops before long, but until then a slightly larger size of clothing proved sufficient.

She tied a Denver Broncos sweatshirt around her neck. They'd be home long before the late afternoon shadows cooled things down, but she wanted to be prepared just in case.

She might even go wading in the lake if it got warm enough. The air had been still that morning and when she'd walked from the office back to her trailer, the sun had felt positively hot.

Checking the grocery sack that held their lunch, she waited impatiently for Mick. She was looking forward to the outing and to the chance to get to know the older man better.

Ten minutes past noon, Dani began to wonder if she'd mixed up the time. Had Mick forgotten? Had something else come up?

She could run next door and see. She was halfway to the door when the knock came. There, he'd just been delayed.

She flung it open, her smile wide and happy. "I thought—"

Dani stopped, her smile fading. Connor stood on her step.

He looked at her, frowning.

"Mick said you needed something carried."

"Where's Mick?"

"He took a run up to Grand Junction. Seems Paul Stephenson and his entourage decided to arrive today. They plan to stay the night in Carson Creek and show up here first thing tomorrow."

"Oh, I thought they were coming after lunch."

"So did we all. Does that pose a problem?"

"No. The office is ready. Thanks for telling me about Mick."

She was disappointed. She'd been looking forward to their picnic.

"What is it you need carried?"

"What? Oh, that." She shrugged, hoping to hide her disappointment.

"Mick and I were going on a picnic. I said I'd fix the food. His contribution was to carry everything. He doesn't think I should lift anything heavier than a pencil, you know."

"A picnic?" Connor said the words as if they were in a foreign language.

"We were going to hike along the lake, find a sunny spot and eat. You know, a picnic? Eat outside?"

"I know what a picnic is, only no one around here goes on them."

"Well, I plan to." She tilted her chin. Just because Mick couldn't come didn't mean she couldn't stick to her plan. The paper bag and blanket weren't all that heavy.

"I'll go with you," Connor said.

Dani blinked. "What?"

That was the last thing she expected.

"To carry things. Unless you don't want me to."

Connor go on a picnic with her? Just the two of them? Consternation threatened. She'd had enough trouble trying to talk to him yesterday.

Not to mention dealing with the curious sensations that swept through her whenever he was near. Such as an increased heart rate and difficulty taking a deep breath.

Even thinking straight!

How would she manage a picnic with the man?

"That would be great." She tried to infuse some enthusiasm into her voice. "Can you spare the time?"

"I don't work 24/7. No one works on Sundays—unless we get too far behind schedule to skip a day off. And so far we're close to being back on target. Besides, I could use a chance to get away. Where's the basket?"

She stepped aside to allow him to enter, gesturing to the bag and blanket on the dining table. He crossed to pick them up.

"It's heavy," he said, tucking the bag in one arm effortlessly, slinging the blanket over one shoulder.

"I didn't know what Mick would like or how much he'd eat, so if anything, I erred on the side of a lot of food. I have three kinds of sandwiches, two kinds of chips, fruit, brownies, colas and napkins and all. Also a bottle of sparkling cider and cups. I, um, thought we could toast a productive meeting with the Windhaven people," she confessed reluctantly.

He'd probably think she was nuts, but she wanted to feel part of the team, and knew Mick would have appreciated her gesture.

"We can leave that here, if you like."

"I like cider."

"Oh."

"You also said brownies? Homemade?"

"Of course. Do you like brownies?"

"I love them. I haven't had any in…" He frowned and headed for the door. "In a long time."

"Which way along the lake is best?" Dani's hands shook a little as she locked her door.

She couldn't believe she was going to have lunch a second day in a row with Connor .

Would he touch her again today? Want to feel the baby if it moved again? Brush back her hair, tangle his fingers in her curls and draw her closer for a kiss?

*A kiss!*

Oh no, she was in trouble if she let her thoughts go in that direction.

Dani shook her head, refusing to give in to fantasy. She hardly knew the man.

He was her boss.

Beside, she'd sworn off involvement and a kiss would surely lead to at least thinking about involvement.

"We'll go to the right," he said, slowing his long strides to accommodate her shorter ones.

Right, in the opposite direction from where he headed after work each day. Where did he go? Was there something to the left he didn't want her to see?

Determined to enjoy herself despite the unease she felt, Dani looked around her.

The lake sparkled in the sunshine. A deep blue, it seemed to stretch on forever. The trees surrounding it were dark green, their trunks rising forty feet or higher. She heard no birds, but could hear squirrels chattering in the branches and in the distance the sound of an animal moving through the underbrush. Deer?

They walked in silence. She vowed she wouldn't be the one to break it. She hadn't asked Connor to accompany her, he'd volunteered. Let him be the one to start the conversation. Anyway, she hadn't a clue what to talk about.

After a while it became harder and harder to keep quiet. She longed to share her enjoyment of the day, exclaim how pretty the lake looked. Share how the stillness fed her soul.

She darted a quick look at Connor. His jaw was set, his eyes narrowed against the sun's glare as he stared straight ahead. Did he even notice where they were? For all the attention he paid, they could be walking through a concrete tunnel.

Dani halted abruptly and held out her hand. "I'll take my lunch and blanket. You can go back."

"What?" He stopped a couple of steps ahead and turned back to look at her. "What are you talking about? I thought we were going on a picnic."

"You look as if you're going to an execution. Picnics are supposed to be fun. I certainly can go by myself. I don't need you to put yourself out to accompany me!"

"I'm not putting myself out to do anything. I haven't eaten lunch. We'll eat what you fixed."

She lowered her hand indecisively. "I know you can't seem to manage a smile, but at least take that scowl off or I'll think you're having a terrible time."

His features relaxed somewhat. "And that's important— what kind of time I'm having?" he asked.

She shrugged. "This is a gorgeous day, we are in a pristine setting. Pretend you're having a good time, if nothing else."

He glanced around at the trees, the lake, then back at her. "I'm enjoying myself."

He said it with a hint of surprise.

"Oh. Well, then. Good."

She smiled and started walking again, almost as surprised as he sounded. A moment later she glanced over her shoulder and found he was still standing where he'd stopped, staring at her legs!

Realizing she'd halted, he looked up and started walking again, catching up with her in three quick strides.

Dani experienced a wave of feminine satisfaction. Often she felt ungainly as she grew larger with her baby. Connor's obvious male appreciation of her legs had her glowing inside.

"How far do you plan to walk before having this feast?" he asked a few minutes later.

"I didn't plan on any set time. I thought when we found a nice spot, we'd just stop."

"There speaks a woman who is either not hungry or too picky for words."

She laughed. "Hungry, huh?"

"Yeah. I keep thinking about those brownies."

"Then how about over there?" She pointed to a wide, picturesque spot on the lake shore. The slope to the lake was gradual. Pine needles cushioning the ground would make it comfortable to sit, and the dappled sunlight would keep them warm but not hot.

He spread out the blanket with little effort and sat on one side, setting the bag in the center. Dani knelt opposite and began to pull the lunch from the bag. She spread it out and let him choose the sandwiches he wanted, the chips. Without a word, she opened the sparkling cider and filled two cups.

"Here's to coming in on schedule and under budget," she said, offering him one and raising hers slightly.

He nodded, taking his paper cup and brushing the edge against hers. Then he drained it.

# Chapter Nine

They ate in companionable silence. Connor raised one knee, resting his arm on it while he used the other hand to eat with. His gaze was on the lake, but from the expression on his face, Dani had a feeling he wasn't enjoying the view.

She was having a great time. She loved listening to the soft lapping of the water and the sounds of nature surrounding them. In the distance she could again hear movement in the underbrush. A hawk lazily circled in the sky. Even the quiet man beside her added to her enjoyment.

Would she ever feel comfortable around him? Not be so aware of his every move, his every expression? Despite his lack of enthusiasm, the day was perfect.

She felt more satisfaction when Connor took a second sandwich.

"It's a nice lunch, Dani. Thanks," he said, catching her gaze on him.

"Thank you for carrying it here. So Mick went to Grand Junction. When did Mr. Stephenson call?"

"Yesterday. The message was on the answering machine when I went into the office after I returned from Carson Creek. Mick volunteered to go pick them up."

"Oh."

He'd had time last night or even this morning before he'd left to let her know of the change in plans. Why hadn't he?

She glanced at Connor. Had Mick hoped she'd accept him as a substitute, and lunch together would help them hammer out their differences so they'd work in better harmony? She should have told Mick they'd had lunch together yesterday. Their relationship was just fine—tenuous, but Connor hadn't fired her yet.

"Do you go on a lot of picnics?" Connor asked.

"No, this is the first in years. It's so beautiful here. Peaceful. I wonder how much it'll change when the resort is fully operational."

"A lot, I'd guess. But that's progress. Come stay sometime when it's open and compare."

"At the rates they'll probably charge, it would be a short stay!"

"Umm." He reached for a brownie.

Dani watched as he savored the chocolate dessert. With a quick glance at her, he took a second one. Then he grew solemn again and stared back at the lake—almost as if he were brooding.

"Is there something wrong?" she asked a few moments later.

He flicked her a glance. "No."

"You don't seem to be exactly enjoying yourself."

"I'm fine."

She watched him for a couple of moments. "Problems on the site?"

"No."

"Worried about Windhaven's inspection?"

"No. Leave it, Dani."

She took a breath, casting around for something else to say.

"Andrews Tool and Die," she exclaimed. "Did you talk to

them?"

He nodded once, abruptly.

"And?"

"And what do you want to know? They were siphoning off funds. We knew that. Any legitimate reasons? No."

"So you'll turn it over to the authorities?"

"Already did, yesterday morning."

"I'm sorry."

He shrugged. After another moment of silence, he spoke. "The thing I can't get over is he thought I'd let it go."

She was startled. "Because of the family ties?"

"Yeah. Because I was married to his sister, he thought I would turn a blind eye to criminal activities."

"He doesn't know you very well, does he?"

Connor looked at her. "What?"

"Dishonesty isn't your strong suit."

Connor stared at her for a long moment, his dark eyes steady. Then he said, "Family loyalty, guilt, whatever—he thought I'd cover for him."

"Where was his family loyalty?" she asked gently. "I don't have family, but even I know you don't cheat your family or friends."

Connor held her gaze for a long moment.

"Good point. He threatened to drag me down with him. He plans to say I was in on it from the beginning."

"As if anyone would believe him. From the few days I've been here, and from the vendors and officials I've spoken with, I know your reputation is sterling. A desperate man—one in the wrong—can sling whatever bull he wants, but it doesn't mean it'll stick."

Connor laughed.

Dani was dumbstruck.

His entire demeanor changed with the laughter. Her heart skipped a beat. He was downright make-your-heart-stop gorgeous. He should smile all the time.

Or maybe not, if he wanted anyone to get anything done. Not that the men would notice, but any woman who saw him would stop everything to soak up that male beauty.

"You're priceless, Dani Winthrop. Sweet and pretty as a summer's day, but such language! It doesn't fit the image."

*Sweet and pretty?*

He thought she was pretty?

She swallowed, suddenly feeling shy. Casting around for something to do, she began to gather up the remnants of the picnic, uncertain whether to be flattered at the description or annoyed that he was laughing at her.

"When plain speaking is needed, I can deliver," she said.

Connor's eyes danced in amusement but he wisely refrained from saying another word.

After she had the things packed away in the bag, he stretched out on the blanket and closed his eyes. Dani gazed dreamily at the water, thinking about his suggestion that she visit after the resort was finished. Could she and her baby come back sometime? When the child was old enough to understand, she could explain how she'd worked on the construction site, could compare the way it would be then with the way it was today. Maybe even come to this very spot with her son or daughter.

And remember her picnic with Connor.

And his compliment.

She'd cherish it all the more, knowing he normally didn't say such things—especially to her. Was this a temporary truce brought on by good weather and brownies?

She glanced at him. He appeared to be asleep. She debated lying down, but eating had refreshed her. After sitting for so long, she found that any tiredness from the walk and morning work had fled. The sun had moved, their filtered shade becoming intense sunshine. She'd tossed her sweatshirt to one side when they began to eat. Now she was growing warmer in just her T-shirt.

The lake beckoned.

She rose and walked to the edge, reaching over to feel the water. Where it was so shallow, it felt warm. Giving in to impulse, she toed off her shoes and pulled off her socks. Stepping gingerly into the water, she wiggled her toes. The pine needles that lined the bottom of the lake disintegrated and drifted around her feet like tiny confetti. Slowly she walked along, watching where she was going, looking for rocks or debris.

Wading a little deeper, she felt the water grow cooler the farther she went. Soon she was up to her knees. She stirred up the muck as she walked, making the water cloudy. It was still crystal clear ahead of her, and she saw a small school of minnows dart one way, then another.

Suddenly she stepped on a rock covered in slime and her foot slipped. Wildly trying to catch her balance, she fell to her hands and knees with a splash that wet the front of her shorts and shirt.

"What do you think you're doing?" Connor roared from behind her.

Dani struggled to get to her feet, her hands and knees stinging. She must have scraped them when she cushioned her fall. But the bottom was slippery and she couldn't get her footing.

Splashing behind her alerted her to Connor's arrival. His strong hands came under her arms and he effortlessly pulled her up, setting her carefully on her feet and then wrapping his arms around her. His arms were like bands of steel, steady and strong. He had her pressed against his hard chest.

The warmth felt good against her damp shirt. She looked up into angry eyes.

"You don't have the sense God gave a mongoose. What do you think you're doing?" he almost yelled.

"Wading. It's hot. I didn't know it would be so slippery."

She clung to him, feeling shaken from her fall. Her wet hands left prints on his shirt. He didn't move his arm and she was grateful for the support.

Her heart raced—a remnant of her fall, or from Connor's proximity?

"I think I can make it to shore," she said, gaining her balance. One step and her foot slipped again. She clutched his arm.

With a short expletive, he swung her into his arms and took three strides, depositing her on the dry shore, water streaming from his shoes and the bottom of his jeans.

"You need a keeper. Stay out of the water! Honestly, no wonder your boyfriend left, you are so much trouble! You needlessly put yourself and that baby at risk. You come to a construction site miles from anywhere—totally inappropriate for a woman, especially a pregnant woman. And then you don't even take care of yourself! What if you'd fallen into a sinkhole? Or hit your head on a rock? You could have drowned!"

He stood, hands on hips, glaring at her as he yelled.

Dani met his gaze unflinchingly. He was right—to a degree—but still overreacting.

And his comment about Marc hurt. He hadn't left because of anything she'd done—except get pregnant.

"I'm fine," she said stiffly. No one had asked Connor to rescue her. She could have managed.

As if she hadn't spoken, he continued, raking his fingers through his hair. "This isn't going to work. I can't worry about a construction site, about the investigation into Pete's embezzlement, and watch over you at the same time!"

"No one asked you to watch over me. Don't worry about me. I've made it this far on my own, and I'll make it the rest of my days on my own."

"And at the rate you're going, the rest of your days will number two! You need to leave, Dani, before something serious happens."

"Don't you dare start that again, Connor. I'm not going anywhere! I'm perfectly okay here. You don't have to nursemaid me or worry. I don't need you or anyone else to act as guardian angel. I'm not your responsibility."

He turned and looked out across the lake, his hands dropping to his sides, clenching into fists.

"Given my track record, maybe that's a good thing."

Without another word, he started walking back to camp.

Dani let him go, watching until he disappeared around the bend. Then she remembered what Mick had said—that Connor felt responsible about not being able to keep his wife and son safe. Was he thinking about them with that last comment?

She walked to her shoes and socks, wringing out as much water from her T-shirt as she could. She scooped up the shoes and took them to the blanket. Sitting, she dried off her feet and legs and put them on. She pulled on the sweatshirt. It was warm from the sun and felt good over her damp clothes.

She'd enjoyed the afternoon—most of it. Folding the blanket, she picked up the picnic bag and rose, wishing she'd handled things differently. Wishing their time together hadn't ended so ignominiously.

Maybe she *had* been a little foolhardy in going wading without knowing more about the situation. And she hadn't needed to go so far out into the water. The ankle-deep shallows had no slippery rocks.

But she was not Connor's responsibility and he had no call to feel she was. Or make a comment about her personal life.

Fat lot he knew. Marc had cut out because of the baby. Though even before that, she'd had uneasy moments. They hadn't been seeing eye to eye on a few other things. His values were not hers.

He was into conspicuous consumption, wearing expensive clothing, taking her to expensive restaurants and making sure they had the best table, and constantly bragging on how much he was making in the stock market.

Dani would have been equally satisfied with walks along Sixteenth Avenue, or taking in a movie, or even a quiet night at home.

Rounding the bend, she saw Connor walking back toward her. Without a word, he reached for the bag and blanket. She relinquished them and took a deep breath.

"I'm sorry for causing you to be upset," she said. "I won't go wading in the future. At least not until after the baby comes. I am taking care of myself. I won't do anything to harm my baby."

He nodded, turning to start back to camp.

"So I stay?" she asked, falling into step with him. She needed that point cleared up.

"At least through Stephenson's visit."

"At least until we close up for winter," she countered.

They walked in awkward silence. Dani longed for the anticipation she'd felt on the outward journey, the joy in the day—not this uneasy tension that shimmered between them.

No tender brushing back her hair today.

No sharing in the baby's movements.

She felt disappointed, discouraged and depressed when she reached her trailer.

He handed her the bag and blanket. "Get into some dry clothes."

She nodded, too dispirited to argue. Did he think she was going to sit around in wet, cold clothes? He could give her a little credit.

"In the future, stay out of trouble. I'm going to take you at your word, that you'll be fine. But you're on your own. Being with you is too much a threat to my sanity."

She watched him walk away again, feeling as low as she had when Marc had told her he wanted nothing to do with the baby.

How could one reckless act ruin her entire day?

And how could she compare Connor's leaving with Marc's?

# Chapter Ten

C onnor entered the office and shut the door behind him. For a moment, he stood still, letting his eyes get used to the dimmer light. His emotions were roiling. He should have told Mick to get one of the other men to carry Dani's things.

Or demanded more of an explanation of what things Mick had been talking about.

And once he'd found out about the picnic, he should have turned and left.

A setup.

Connor knew one when he saw it. His partner was doing all he could to convince him Dani Winthrop should remain. But Connor didn't know how much longer he could put up with the turmoil she caused.

He'd been fine these last couple of years. Going through the motions of work, finding solace in the twilight hours before dinner. The searing pain of losing Catherine and Sammy had eased. And he'd been able to get through each day.

He'd definitely not been disturbed by flashes of a beguiling smile or blond hair that had him itching to find out if those curls would wrap themselves around a man's fingers and never let go.

He walked to his desk, sat down and surveyed the office with a scowl. Frowning he had to admit she was good at her job.

It would be so much easier if she fit his first expectation—an air head intent on flirting with every man on the project.

Instead, she'd knuckled down and pushed to get the office organized. Had ignored the men on the project. And raised havoc in his own mind.

The office was the cleanest he'd ever seen it. She'd done a great job preparing for the meeting. Why couldn't she just focus on that—do her work, rest in her trailer? Stay out of his way.

Why go to lunch in Carson Creek in a dress that looked like soft sunshine?

Why talk about a little backwater town with wonder and delight in her voice?

Or share her story of a childhood that sounded bleak and loveless?

So different from his.

Yet they'd both ended up in the same place, running from the blows life had dealt.

It should establish a bond between them.

But he didn't want any bond. Any connection. His life was going the way he wanted—no complications, no demands, no responsibilities for another person, just the work at hand.

He'd already failed once—failed to keep his wife and child safe. Failed to keep his own heart from shattering.

He wasn't strong enough to try again.

He reached for the thick folder that had all the reports for Paul Stephenson. Work had gotten him through Catherine's and Sammy's deaths. Work would get him through this.

Only two months remained until he and Mick planned to shut down for the winter. He could last two months by focusing strictly on work. Ignore the soft feminine body that was so enticing when Dani walked beside him. Ignore the fantastic legs that had almost had him drooling earlier in the day. Forget his fascination with her hair.

Ignore, refute, deny the awakening he felt when she was near, when he smelled her sweet scent, when she smiled at him and all the joy of the day shone in her eyes.

Two months. He could hold out for two months.

On Monday morning Dani dressed in her new jeans and boots. A loose T-shirt beneath her flannel shirt gave her the option of removing the flannel shirt later if she got too warm. She did her best with her hair, taming it slightly beneath a wide band. Studying herself in the mirror, she hoped she looked competent and rugged—totally suitable to be secretary on a remote construction site.

She couldn't deal with Mr. Stephenson also siding with Connor in wanting her to go.

For a moment, she considered not showing up. But that wouldn't be professional. She wouldn't let Mick down like that.

She was one of the team, and now she looked the part.

She was at her desk by eight.

Connor didn't show up until the entourage from Windhaven arrived. He'd been over every inch of the construction area to make sure it would show well if Stephenson wanted a tour.

Mick entered first, congenially waving the others into the office.

A tall, thin man with gray hair entered next. His dark suit looked out of place to Dani after a week of seeing jeans and hard hats. His shirt was snowy white, his tie a dark red.

Following him was a younger man carrying a briefcase in one hand and laptop bag in the other. He, too, sported a dark suit and power tie.

The third member of the Windhaven group was a woman. Tall and slender with short, dark hair, she was dressed in a charcoal-gray suit, the skirt of which barely came to mid thigh, showing off spectacular legs. The high heel shoes she wore emphasized the long length of those legs. No blouse, just a hint of lace at the deep V of the jacket. It was the perfect look for a woman on the move up.

Or on the prowl, Dani thought with a surprising spurt of cattiness. Connor had best watch out for *her* distracting the men!

The woman's makeup was flawless, her composure confident. Her gaze darted everywhere, taking in everything. She spotted Dani and a finely plucked eyebrow rose.

Connor brought up the rear and closed the door.

Introductions were quickly made. Deirdre Evans represented the PR department of Windhaven. She gave Dani a quick, insincere smile.

Paul Stephenson showed no surprise at meeting Dani. Mick must have filled him in on her status on the ride from Grand Junction.

George Peters, the accountant, scarcely acknowledged her presence. He was too busy setting up his laptop.

"I didn't realize you had a woman secretary," Deirdre said to Connor when everyone sat around the long, makeshift conference table Dani had prepared for the meeting. Deirdre drew her own chair slightly closer to Connor than Dani had placed them. "That doesn't cause complications?"

Dani remained at her desk. She was not needed for this meeting, but couldn't disappear. She had work to do. And wanted to be ready if they needed more coffee or pencils sharpened.

"She hasn't been here long," Connor said shortly.

Dani almost held her breath, but he didn't add that she'd be leaving soon. Or that she wreaked havoc on the site. But he said nothing further.

"It must be so interesting to work in what's traditionally a man's field," Deirdre said across the room to Dani.

"Actually, I'm the secretary—traditionally a woman's field. I don't work on the actual construction, just in the office."

Deirdre smiled again and dismissed her.

Obviously seeing me as no competition, Dani thought wryly. She couldn't blame her. Maybe today wasn't the most auspicious day to have worn her jeans. On the other hand, her loose dresses did not convey sleek sophistication. In that field, Deirdre won hands down.

Try as she might as the morning progressed, Dani was unable to ignore the others to concentrate on her own duties. She'd find herself listening to the conversations, glancing up once in a while—usually when Connor was speaking. Just to learn more about the project, she assured herself, gazing at his confident presentation and response to any and all questions posed.

She wasn't the only one. Deirdre virtually ignored the others at the table, focusing exclusively on Connor. Of course, she already knew her Windhaven colleagues. Was this her first time meeting Connor or did she always behave that way?

If she thought she could get away with it, she'd probably drape herself over his arm and latch on, Dani thought as she divided her attention between Connor and Deirdre, growing frustrated.

She was not jealous, she told herself, just watching out for her boss. Any competent secretary would do so.

As lunchtime drew near, Paul Stephenson said he wanted to return to Carson Creek to eat. Dani noticed that neither Mick nor Connor voiced any opposition. Were they glad for the break? Or was the meeting concluding?

"I'll ride with Connor," Deirdre said, smiling at him provocatively. "He can tell me more about the area. I need more information to fully exploit the potential in our marketing strategy."

Dani had her own ideas on what Deirdre wanted to fully exploit.

From the look on Connor's face, Dani suspected the last thing he wanted was to be alone with the woman for any length of time—much less the duration of the ride to Carson Creek.

"Oh, I'm sorry. Connor, did you forget that call that's coming in at noon? It's really important—from Jasper," Dani interjected. He could take the lifeline or not, but she'd done her best.

He looked at her and nodded, taking a deep breath. "I had forgotten it was today. I'll have to skip lunch." He looked at Paul. "When you get back, we'll cover the site. You can see the progress and ask any other questions that arise."

Connor stood, on the far side of his chair from Deirdre, and nodded to her. "Dani can show you around after lunch. You shouldn't be in the actual construction zone in those shoes you're wearing."

Paul stacked his reports and left them in a pile at his place. "We'll be back around three. A brief tour will be enough. We assessed the progress when we drove in. Deirdre, you might want to get a woman's perspective of this place by talking to Dani. Get her to show you what she likes here."

Deirdre was definitely not pleased, but she kept her

composure and nodded agreeably, with only her flashing eyes indicating her annoyance. "I'm a woman, in case you forgot, Paul. But another's view would be helpful, I'm sure."

Dani knew that had not been Deirdre's plan. Any comments she herself offered would probably be ignored. Deirdre had already made her disinterest known.

Once Mick and the Windhaven group left, Connor leaned against his desk, crossed his arms over his chest and looked at Dani.

"I owe you—big-time."

"Not up to lunch with Deirdre?"

"Or the ride in. What a shark, sleek and deadly. Who's Jasper?"

Dani smiled and shrugged. "I haven't a clue. The name just popped into mind. But a good secretary knows when to throw her boss a lifeline."

He nodded. "I'll keep that in mind. Are you up to showing Deirdre around this afternoon? I probably should have asked you before volunteering your services."

"But it was do-or-die time. That's fine. We can walk to the lake. Even in those shoes she's wearing." Dani didn't say any more about the inappropriateness of the woman's attire for reviewing a construction site.

"However," she said, "something tells me she'll want a tour by the top dog of where the lobby will be, so she can write something wonderful about the view. And where the pool will be, so she can rhapsodize about its gem of a setting and where the—"

"I get it. If she makes a fuss, Mick gets that assignment. Jasper's going to dump something big that I need to deal with immediately." His eyes held amusement as he studied Dani.

"Pete never thought so fast on his feet."

"He had other priorities, I suspect," she said dryly.

The amusement left Connor's face. "So he did. You look different today."

"I've tamed my hair as much as I can and I'm wearing jeans."

"Why?"

She blinked. She thought he'd appreciate her looking more like she belonged on the site.

"To blend in, so you wouldn't even notice I was here," she said slowly, wondering if she were revealing too much.

He shook his head. "Never happen."

He straightened and headed for the door. "Take lunch. They'll be back far too soon for my peace of mind. I'm going out to make sure everything's ready for the great inspection."

Dani nodded, watching him leave. Her heart skipped a beat. She'd done good and he knew it.

And she'd continue to do good, she vowed after lunch, when she and Deirdre were making their way down to the lake shore. She'd give the woman no excuse to complain about her to Connor.

Deirdre looked everywhere but where she was going. When one of the workers gave a wolf whistle, she smiled and waved, almost preening.

Dani rolled her eyes. Not too discerning, she thought. And just the type of woman Connor did not want on the site. Deirdre probably relished setting men on end.

"So are you pregnant or just a little pudgy?" Deirdre asked once they'd left the building behind them.

"Pregnant," Dani replied quietly.

Tact wasn't Deirdre's strong point, either.

"Poor you. Is that why you are here, in the back of beyond—because your husband works on the site?"

"No." Dani had no intention of telling this woman anything about her life.

"Then?"

"For the money," she said, suspecting that would be an explanation Deirdre would understand. It was.

"Ah, combat pay? They would have to pay extra to entice anyone out here, I'd think. Carson Creek is not exactly Chicago."

Dani made no reply. Let the woman think what she would. Dani was growing to love working here. The setting was perfect, the job interesting and never boring. But she suspected Deirdre would never see it that way.

Mick was a great boss—gave her directions, then let her do the work without micro management.

Connor...well, nothing in life was perfect.

"Is Connor Norris married?" Deirdre asked abruptly.

"No."

They reached the lake. Dani gazed at the beauty and felt the serenity almost envelop her. She was not going to gossip about her boss.

"Living with anyone?"

"What?"

"Connor," Deirdre said impatiently. "Is he involved with someone?"

Dani shook her head. "Not interested, I think."

"Oh, men are always interested—with the right woman."

Dani thought about Marc. He'd be interested—more than interested—if Deirdre threw a lure out his way. For a moment Dani wondered if she could introduce the two of them. If ever two people deserved each other, it would be Deirdre and Marc.

"Do you want to walk along the shore?" Dani asked.

"What's there to see that we haven't already seen? Once the resort is up and running, there'll be plenty of activity, but right now it's water and trees."

"It's quieter if we walk that way. The view is different. Once we round that bend over there, we can't see or hear the construction and the lake really opens up so we can see down the full length of it."

"Why bother? A lake is a lake. I've seen enough. I'd get a better impression of things from the building. See what guests would see from the lobby, that kind of thing."

Dani hid a smile as they turned and walked back. "Have you been doing this kind of work for long?"

"A couple of years. Windhaven is an international firm, you know. My goal is Europe. But I have to work my way up. If I do a great job with this project, I'll be in a better position to request my own assignment next time. Let's stop back in the office. Maybe Connor is through with whatever he had to do and he can show me the building site. Better than risking you showing me, in your condition and all," Deirdre said.

As if that was the reason, Dani thought wryly.

George, the accountant, was busily comparing reports with data on his computer when they entered. Connor and the others were not present. Deirdre frowned. "Where's Connor?" she asked her colleague.

"He and Mick are showing Paul something," George said vaguely, not taking his eyes from his computer.

Deirdre gave an exclamation of frustration and reached out to snag one of the extra hard hats from a hook near the door.

"I'll find them. Thanks for showing me around," she said to Dani.

Placing the hat on her head at a cocky angle, she walked out.

"Maybe I should go with her," Dani said aloud, wondering how far she'd get before Connor saw her. Would he hold her responsible for turning Deirdre loose?

"She can find her way," George murmured. "Or get someone to help her. She's good at that."

Dani went to her desk and sat. There was always plenty to do without baby-sitting visitors.

# Chapter Eleven

It was almost dark by the time Connor returned to the office. "Paul's ready to leave," he told George.

From the look of frustration on his face, he'd had enough of Windhaven's inspection. He glanced at Dani.

"Deirdre find you?" she asked.

"Mick gave her a tour of the site. She said she has enough information to write a draft. Then she'll ask for our input. Like I know anything about publicity or marketing."

"Can I take this last batch of invoices with me?" George asked. "I didn't get through as much as I thought I would."

"Dani can make copies for you of anything you want. We always send attachments when billing," Connor replied.

"I know, but this would give me a head start."

"Fine. I'll tell Paul you'll be out in a few minutes."

Connor turned to leave.

Dani joined Connor in front of the office twenty minutes later as Mick prepared to drive Paul, Deirdre and George to Carson Creek. He was staying in town with the Windhaven group and would take them to Grand Junction for their flight the next morning.

"Did it go well?" she asked as the car pulled away.

"As good as it gets, I guess," Connor replied. "At least they don't plan to return until spring, unless something major turns up."

"Like a new view from the lobby," Dani said quietly.

Connor sighed and nodded. "Man, I'm beat. Dealing with them is worse than working in the pouring rain. I'm heading for home."

Dani watched him walk away, then turned to close the office.

Bill and Moose waved. Tommy called a greeting as she headed for her own trailer.

She was gradually getting to know the men. But, ever conscious of Connor's views, she made no attempt to develop a friendship with anyone.

She passed Connor's trailer on the way to hers. Would he take his walk along the lake this late? It was almost dark. Before long he wouldn't be able to see much without a flashlight.

Though with the tough day behind him, he might long for the solitude of the lake shore.

As she let herself into her trailer, she had an idea. She could take him some more of the brownies she'd made on Saturday.

If not, she'd end up eating them all, and she didn't need the extra pounds—especially after Deirdre's comment.

Dani went directly to the kitchen to fill a small plate with brownies. Covering them with plastic wrap, she hesitated. He wouldn't see this as fawning, would he?

Before she could let doubt rule, she headed out. If he'd gone for his walk, she could always bring the brownies back home, or leave them on his steps.

Connor opened the door at her hesitant knock.

"I thought you might like something special after the all-day meeting. There's nothing like chocolate to perk someone up!"

she said, offering the plate.

He looked at the plate and then at Dani. After a moment, he stood aside and opened the door wider. "Come in."

The second Dani stepped inside, she saw that his trailer was newer, bigger and better furnished than hers. Which made sense—it was his home. Had he bought it after his wife died? Or had Catherine helped?

Dani spotted the kitchen and veered there to deposit the brownies.

It was when she walked back into the living room that she saw the photo—an eight-by-ten of a woman and child. Obviously Connor's family.

With a quick glance at him, she walked to the picture and picked it up. Catherine had had short black hair and dark eyes that seemed to smile directly at her. Sammy had been a darling little boy, complete with a cowlick in the back of his dark hair and a smattering of freckles across his nose.

"School picture. They got a joint one because she taught there and he'd just started kindergarten. Taken two weeks before they were killed," Connor said tightly from behind her. "It arrived in the mail the day of the funeral."

Dani fought down the ache that his words brought. Slowly she replaced the picture on the end table. "I'm so sorry."

"Yeah, everybody's sorry. Doesn't bring them back."

Dani wished she could say something to make a difference, but she did not have any words to ease his pain. Nothing would bring back his wife and son.

"I'd better go."

She turned and started for the door. There was nothing for her at her trailer—no memories, few regrets and a lonely dinner.

What did Connor have? Not much more—poignant

memories, a lingering regret over circumstances he couldn't alter.

"Want to eat dinner here?" he asked when her hand touched the doorknob.

Dani glanced at him in surprise. Connor had invited her to stay?

"It's not much, just spaghetti. Sauce from a jar, but lots of it. And garlic bread," he said. Standing across the room from her, he looked uncertain, lonely.

Her heart was touched. And she'd appreciate the company.

"Sounds wonderful."

Where had that invitation come from? Connor wondered as soon as the words left his mouth. What was he doing, inviting her to stay?

From the smile that touched her lips, she was delighted. He was a fool!

"What can I do to help?" she asked.

He frowned. What had he started?

"I can manage, unless you want a salad. I don't have anything for that."

"I do. How about I go and fix a salad and come back in about twenty minutes?"

"Fine."

Reprieve.

He watched her go, then headed to the kitchen. He got tired of eating alone night after night. He often called Mick and the two of them threw something together. Dani was just another co-worker—someone to share a meal with. No big deal.

As he began to prepare the meal, he tried to keep his mind blank, or focus on the day's meeting. It had gone well despite Deirdre and her flirtatious ways. Even the latest discovery about Andrews Tool and Die had been mentioned and dismissed.

Windhaven had not borne the brunt of the embezzlement, J&J Construction had. The resort owners were satisfied with the way he and Mick were handling things.

Dani had been an asset, as she probably knew. He almost smiled when he remembered her clever trick, giving him an out for lunch.

For that and the brownies, he owed her.

Dinner was simply a way to repay the favor. It wasn't as if they were going out on a date or anything. But dinner with a fellow worker–he did that all the time with Mick.

But Mick didn't disturb his equilibrium. Didn't bring long-dormant interest and awareness alive. Didn't have his blood thrumming through his veins when he laughed, or glanced up with bright blue eyes.

Catherine's eyes had been dark. As had Sammy's.

Dani was nothing like Catherine.

He sliced the bread, smeared garlic butter on both sides and wrapped it in aluminum foil.

For a moment, he couldn't picture Catherine. He looked at the photo in the living room. There. She was there, as pretty as she'd ever been. As pretty as she would always be.

He couldn't forget her. They'd been together most of their lives. It felt like a betrayal to even think of another woman.

*Move on, Connor.*

The words sounded so clearly in his mind he almost dropped the knife.

He had moved on.

He'd sold their home, unable to bear staying in it with both of them gone. He had made a life for himself, working with Mick on remote sites—sites a lot of other construction firms didn't want because of the challenges inherent in out-of-the-way places and the distances from home.

Home was now this trailer. It went where he went.

If a man traveled lightly, he couldn't get bogged down in relationships, nor risk his heart again.

The knock on the door came too soon. He took a breath and went to open it and let Dani in. Her smile was tentative, as if she wasn't sure of his welcome. He nodded, tried to remember the rules of polite behavior.

"I brought two bottles of dressing, not knowing which you'd like. But there are lots of good veggies in the salad. I like fresh veggies, but they're hard to get this late in the season."

"I don't bother with salads much. But this looks great. Thanks."

Her smile became more relaxed and she followed him into the kitchen.

"I thought we'd eat at the counter." It was less formal. Where he and Mick ate. Less like a date.

"Fine. Shall I get the silverware?"

"In that drawer." He pointed and headed back to the stove.

In only a short time, Connor served up the food, heaping plates with noodles and sauce.

"I know I'm eating for two, but this is about a week's worth of food," she protested when he set her plate before her.

"Eat what you want. I'm used to Mick's appetite."

Connor's own plate was piled higher.

He took some of the salad, more to be polite than anything. Catherine had been big on salads, too. Was that a woman thing? Pouring on the dressing, he ate without speaking. Dani had put a lot into the mix—tomatoes, green peppers, mushrooms, celery, carrots and two kinds of lettuce. It was good.

She ate the spaghetti quietly, not speaking.

After Deirdre's clinging and posturing that day, it proved a refreshing change.

But even though Dani didn't speak, he was aware of her. Her scent, light and sweet, seemed to subtly infiltrate his space. Her skin was fair, with faint color just below the surface. She was still in her jeans and flannel shirt, but made them look sexy instead of functional.

He scowled and looked away. He was not thinking sexy!

Her hair seemed to dance around her head as she looked around, taking in everything about his home.

What did she think about it? It was more luxurious than her own, but still a temporary abode. No pictures except of Catherine and Sammy. None of the knickknacks women seemed to favor.

"It's delicious," Dani said after a while. "Do you and Mick often eat together?"

"As often as not. It saves one of us cooking each night. I especially like it the nights he cooks."

"Because you take a walk to the lake every day?"

He glanced at her. "I like some quiet time after the workday." He hesitated a moment, then continued. "Catherine and I always spent time together before dinner."

"That's a nice tradition. I expect you miss that routine." Her voice was kind, but not dripping with sympathy.

He nodded. When he was at the lake he could almost imagine Catherine was nearby, would be coming to join him momentarily.

"What was she like?" she asked.

"Catherine?"

"Yes. She was pretty, I can see that from the picture. She reminds me of someone, but I can't think who. Was she tall, short, what?"

"She was tall, five feet ten inches. When she wore high heel shoes, she was almost as tall as I am."

Dani stifled a sigh. She'd always longed to be tall and svelte. Tall and thin and sophisticated—like Catherine. And Deirdre.

She sat up. "Deirdre, that's who Catherine reminds me of. They look a little alike, don't you think? And Deirdre is tall."

"No, they darn well do not look alike! Deirdre is nothing like Catherine," he said.

It was preposterous.

Yet after that knee-jerk reaction, he reflected. Maybe he could see how an outsider might think that. Tall, sleek black hair, slender—there was a superficial resemblance, maybe. Deirdre dressed with more sophistication then Catherine ever had. And while there might be some slight physical similarity, there was none in attitude or personality.

"Umm, I think they look a bit alike," Dani repeated.

She was not one to back down.

Connor nodded reluctantly.

"Maybe generally, in physical looks, but they are nothing alike otherwise."

The same way neither was like Dani Winthrop. She was a unique individual, carving a life for herself despite setbacks and a wobbly start. How did she keep that sunny disposition with all that had happened?

He wished he knew more about her, without having to ask. He didn't want to give the impression he was interested in more than a employer-employee relationship.

Maybe Mick knew more about Dani, Connor mused.

Had he himself forgotten how to talk with people outside of work? He suspected if he just asked the right questions, she'd open up and share without reservation. And without expectations.

Her hand reached for another piece of garlic bread at the same time his did. Her fingers brushed against his and she jerked back as if she'd been stung.

He lifted the plate and offered her a piece, still feeling the fleeting touch of her fingers. He studied her hands—slender fingers, nails short and lacquered with clear polish. Not the red talons Deirdre sported. For a moment the thought popped into his mind: what would they feel like touching him?

Watching warily, she took a slice and put it on her plate. She seemed uncomfortable. He took his own piece of bread, trying to think up something to say to ease the rising tension. He had no business thinking of touching or softness or anything about the woman beside him. He should never have invited her to dinner.

"—every winter?"

Connor looked away. What was she talking about? How had he lost track of the conversation?

"What?"

"What are you going to do when you shut down the site for winter? Do you build smaller projects in southern climates? Take a long vacation? Or do you just stop work every winter?"

"Mick and I plan to stay in Carson Creek this winter, to be near the site. Once the snow comes, the road into here will be impassable until spring. We need to get the trailers out before then. We'll use Carson Creek as a base for winter. We have two satellite projects going. I'll spend some time in Boulder and Mick will probably check in on the one in Pueblo. The winter months will pass quickly. The sooner we can get back on-site next spring, the better."

"I'm not certain yet where I'll settle. I've lived in Denver most of my life but I don't want to go back there. I always wanted to live in the country. A smaller town would be better to raise a baby, I think."

"What about the father? Isn't this a long way for him to see the baby?"

"As far as Marc is concerned, the baby is not his concern. He disavowed any knowledge."

She'd never forget how he'd reacted when she told him—demanding she get rid of it, swearing she'd tricked him, that he had no intention of tying himself down with anyone at this point in his life, especially a baby!

"But it is his?"

"Oh, yes. There's no doubt there."

"There's always DNA testing, if you need proof."

She nodded. "I've thought about it, but decided not to push the issue. If he wants nothing to do with the baby, so be it. I'm not going to force the issue. It saves problems down the road. And I can manage."

"What if something happens to you?"

"That's my worst nightmare. That something will happen to me and this baby will be alone in the world. It's an awful feeling when you realize you have no family, no one to count on to help in an emergency," Dani said slowly.

Connor imagined that for someone raised unhappily in foster care, it would be a terrifying thought to contemplate for her own baby.

"Chances are you'll live to be ninety or older."

"Hold that thought!" she said, trying to smile.

"No grandparents, aunts, uncles or other family around?"

"No one. As I told you at lunch the other day, I'm alone in

the world until my baby comes. Then we'll be a family."

Connor thought about his own family. He hadn't seen his parents since he'd sold his house. But he talked with them every few months. Kept in touch. Sort of.

His brother was up in Alaska, but Connor still dropped him a card now and then.

And he had aunts and uncles and cousins scattered all over Colorado. If he ever needed anything, he had family who would rally around.

As they had when Catherine and Sammy had been killed.

Dani had no one.

For a moment a strong protective surge overtook him. He wanted to offer her assurance that she'd be okay. That if anything went wrong, she could call on him.

He stared at his empty plate, stunned at the very thought. A week before, he'd flat out said she needed to leave. Now he thought about offering help if she ran into trouble?

No way.

Dinner was drawing to a close. He'd thank her for the salad and brownies and send her on her way. In the future, late or not, he'd take his walk to the lake and revel in the solitary time before dinner.

"Great dinner, but I can't eat another bite," she said, laying down her fork and pushing the plate a little away. "Thank you for asking me to stay. It gets a bit lonely sometimes. Not that I'm complaining. I love working here."

"But you must miss friends."

"A little. I wrote them about this place. And if I settle in Carson Creek, I'll get wifi and be able to email and Skype. How about you? How do you keep up with friends?"

He rose and cleared their places. "I don't—too busy with

work."

He'd cut off all overtures from his friends, swamped by their sympathy. It had been years since he'd left Fort Collins. He'd lost touch with almost everyone.

Except Marshal Andrews, Catherine's brother, and look where that had gone.

"A person is better off on his own," Connor murmured, running water in the sink.

"I agree. I know I can count on myself. Why make friends who will let you down, or turn on you?" She stepped up beside him, scarcely coming to his shoulder. Even though a wide band held her hair back from her face, short wisps of golden hair framed her face. He missed the frame of locks around her cheeks. He'd like to slip the band off and let her hair spring free.

She reached out to take a plate from him. "I can wash the dishes. It's the least I can do after that great dinner. But you have to put them away because I don't know where they go."

He shut off the water. She was standing too close. Her light fragrance filled the air. He could feel the warmth from her body, see the sparkling blue of her eyes.

He wanted to kiss her. Wanted to feel that petite body pressed against him, her arms around his neck, her mouth opened beneath his.

He really, really wanted to kiss Dani Winthrop, until they both forgot their names or where they were. Forgot the past and the future and embraced the moment.

The thought scared him to death.

Connor took her by the shoulders and marched her from the kitchen. Even through the flannel shirt, he could feel the softness of her skin.

Was he nuts? He felt flannel, that was all. Warm from her

body, but cotton only. No silky soft skin. No texture like velvet.

"I'll clean up. You need to go home."

"I do?"

"Get some rest. You look tired. Today was hectic. Tomorrow we'll have to play catch-up on what didn't get done today."

The hurt in her eyes almost made him change his mind. Almost, but not quite. Not if he wanted to keep his sanity.

"Good night. Thanks for dinner."

Her voice sounded bruised.

"Thanks for the brownies." He opened the door, impatient for her to leave. Wanting her to leave before he forgot himself and drew her into his arms. Before he shut off the lights and let the two of them go where the urge would take them.

# Chapter Twelve

Dani walked back to her trailer feeling totally confused. What had just happened? She thought they'd enjoyed a nice meal together. But once finished, he couldn't get her out of his place fast enough.

Had it been the talk of friendship? Did he think she wanted more from him than a strictly boss-secretary relationship?

Maybe she should go back and clarify that.

She hesitated a moment, decided against it and continued to her trailer. Once she reached her temporary home, she did her best to put all thought of the man from her mind. Expunge every memory cell. Forget trying to figure the man out. He was unfigurable.

And he'd been right; she was tired. An early night would be great, recharge her for tomorrow.

Of course, trying to ignore the man insured that he was at the forefront of her thoughts. She remembered every word he'd ever said. Remembered being carried from the lake shore, being scooped up when she'd fallen wading. Remembered the feel of his hands on her shoulders as he'd turned her away from the sink.

Remembered the play of light in the office when he worked. And visualized him striding around the site, hard hat on,

SWEET MEANT TO BE | 121

directing the men and equipment, ruler of his own kingdom.

She was not going to succumb to fantasies about Connor Norris. He'd made his position clear—very clear.

*He still loved his wife.*

And Dani was wise enough to know her own judgment of others was skewed. Maybe because of her up-bringing or maybe because of a defective gene. Who knew? But her track record wasn't impressive. He was not interested in her and she had no business wondering more about him.

How long would he grieve for his wife? How lonely he must be in the evenings, alone in that trailer. What were his plans for the future? Whatever they were, they wouldn't include her.

She had seven more weeks to work with him, weather permitting, that was all. Nothing to get excited about and certainly nothing to count on. She was the only one she could count on. Marc had hammered that lesson home!

The next morning passed swiftly. Dani had plenty to do. Thanks to a restless night, she wasn't functioning in top form. Grateful when the lunch break arrived, she hurried to her trailer. Making a quick sandwich, she sank onto the sofa, relishing the relief as she leaned back. She'd close her eyes just for a moment. Then she'd eat.

While she'd gone right to bed after returning last night, she'd tossed and turned all night long, feeling afterward as if she'd had very little sleep. Only a small portion could be attributed to an active baby. Mostly she lay awake with restless thoughts about Connor. She hadn't felt this way before and didn't know how to handle it.

It felt so good now, to just relax.

At one-fifteen, Connor glanced at his watch for the third time. Mick was on the phone. Dani was not at her desk. In the week she'd been with them, she'd been prompt on every occasion. What was taking her so long this lunch hour?

He put on his hard hat and headed for the door. Mick glanced up but continued to listen to the vendor on the other end of the phone.

The day was warm, the sun shining in a cloudless sky. The long-range forecast had predicted a storm later in the week. But with any luck, it'd rain on Saturday and be clear again by next Monday.

Connor stood in front of the office for a moment, scanning the work site. Men went about their accustomed jobs. The crane had placed the last piling yesterday, Moose showing off his expertise for the visitors. No one slacked off on Connor's site.

So where was Dani?

Taking a breath, he turned and headed for her trailer. Had she just let the time slip away or had something happened to her? Again?

He knocked and waited. Nothing. Knocking again, he called her name. Still no reply.

Trying the knob, he found the door unlocked. Opening it, he stepped inside.

She was sound asleep on the sofa, her feet resting on a chair pulled in front of her. Beside her on the cushion was a plate with a sandwich. She hadn't even taken a bite.

"Dani?" he called softly.

She didn't respond.

He remembered when Catherine had been pregnant with Sammy, how tired she'd been. She'd complained she could hardly wait for school to end each day so she could take a nap. Then she'd be good for the rest of the evening.

He lifted the plate from the sofa and took it into the kitchen. Walking into Dani's bedroom, he paused at the doorway, scanning the tiny room. It was as neat as a pin. She obviously made the bed before going to work. There was nothing feminine or frilly about the room. She even used the bedding the company provided. But the air held her fragrance, and the small closet spilled over with the pastel dresses she'd worn last week.

He drew the spread from the bed and returned to the living room. Draping it over the back of the chair, he reached out to shift her position until she was lying down. She mumbled, then fell quiet, still asleep. He slipped her shoes from her feet. With the jeans she wore, she probably didn't need a covering, but he covered her, anyway.

Her cheeks were slightly flushed, her lashes looking like dark semicircles above them. She seemed younger without that feisty determination facing him.

Slowly Connor reached out and touched the shimmering blond tresses, soft as down. Gently he wrapped a curl around his finger, fascinated by the degree of softness. He would have thought hair that fine would have no body to hold a curl.

He unwound the curl and turned.

What was he doing? She was an employee. And one that had caused him more trouble since she'd arrived than all the others on-site combined.

He walked out and quietly closed the door behind him.

Heading for the office, he entered a minute later to find Mick gone.

Quickly writing a note, he left it on Dani's desk and left. He had work to do.


Dani came awake slowly. She wished she could turn over and

sleep in. But today wasn't Saturday.

Today was Tuesday.

She sat up.

Tuesday afternoon!

"Oh, *no!*" she wailed, jumping up and untangling herself from the spread. She stopped and looked at it. Had she brought that out? She didn't remember.

Looking around, she spotted her sandwich on the counter in her kitchen. She knew she'd brought it to the sofa. Slipping on her shoes, she had a sinking feeling someone had been inside her trailer. She didn't remember taking her shoes off.

She looked at the clock. It was almost three! Panicked, she dashed out of the trailer and almost ran to the office. If Connor needed any excuse to fire her, this would give him a doozy!

How could she have fallen asleep at lunch? She knew she had to be back by one.

Had someone come to her place? Had she slept through someone entering and then covering her with the spread?

She rushed into the office, excuses trembling on her lips. The place was empty.

Going to the window, Dani looked out. She didn't see Connor or Mick, just the men working. She recognized one or two. The rest she hadn't sorted out yet.

Turning, she went to her desk. She saw the note before she sat down.

"Dani—plan to stay late today. Take a longer lunch hour. We'll work past six." It was signed "Connor."

She sat down slowly. Take a longer lunch hour?

He knew! It had to have been Connor who'd covered her up. But if so, why hadn't he woken her, told her to show up on time or be fired?

Maybe it had been Mick.

For the moment, she didn't care. Her job was still safe.

She had to make sure that didn't happen again!

Of course, if she got a decent night's sleep, it wouldn't. She felt tired during the day, but her doctor had told her to expect that. Normally she could handle it by going to bed early at night.

She began to work, hoping she could get things under control before Mick or Connor returned.

It was late afternoon when Dani decided to call the local doctor for an appointment. Her obstetrician had told her to have biweekly checkups as she moved into the last trimester of pregnancy.

She was able to get an appointment late on Friday afternoon. Hopefully it would not be a problem taking off early from work. She could always make up some of the missed time on Saturday.

When she noticed the men drifting by the office, quitting for the day, her trepidation rose slightly. Connor would be back. Had he been the one? Or Mick? She wished she knew.

Mick entered the office and dropped a stack of blueprints on his desk.

"It's hot as blazes midday, yet the temp drops so much by this time of day I need a jacket," he grumbled.

"It's amazing how nice the weather's been," Dani said, wondering how to broach the subject of lunch.

"Yeah, well, I heard a storm's expected this weekend."

"Not Friday?" She didn't relish driving that dirt track in a rainstorm. It would become a sea of mud!

"Naw, Saturday I think. Connor hopes it'll blow through fast enough to be dry again by Monday. I hope so, too."

He looked at her closely. "You okay?"

"I'm fine." Dani smiled brightly. "Why?"

"Thought you'd be winding up for the day. It's after five."

"Connor left me a note, saying he needed me to stay late tonight."

"Why?"

"I don't know, but I don't mind. I took a longer lunch hour than usual."

She held her breath, but Mick said nothing.

Darn, if it wasn't Mick, she'd bet her last dollar Connor had found her asleep.

"I would like to take off early on Friday, if I may. I have a doctor's appointment."

"Something is wrong," Mick said, jumping to conclusions.

"No. Pregnant women get regular checkups. My obstetrician in Denver recommended a doctor here and I made an appointment for Friday. It's routine. Nothing to worry about. But I'll need to leave by three to get there in time."

"Fine. Let Connor know."

She nodded, rather wishing Mick would tell him.

"You two getting along?" Mick asked.

Dani nodded again. She thought they were. Didn't dinner at Connor's place qualify as getting along?

And so far he hadn't fired her for falling asleep in the middle of the day.

Mick smiled. "I knew he'd come around. That boy isn't dumb."

Dani hid a smile. Connor most definitely was no boy!

She was glad to get Mick's okay for Friday. She found it much easier to deal with Mick than with his partner!

"Sonny caught a mess of fish yesterday, so some of the boys are throwing a fish fry tonight. Want to join us?" Mick asked.

"No, thanks."

She had no wish to get tangled up with the others on-site. Despite her nap, she wanted to go to bed early.

"Maybe another time," Mick said, heading for the door.

Dani was noncommittal. She could see the wisdom of Connor's edict. She spoke occasionally with Bill and Tommy. But they sought her out, she didn't look for them.

Other than that, she was friendly, waved if waved to and smiled at everyone. But that was her limit of interaction—totally superficial!

Except for her boss and lunch. And dinner. And a picnic.

Maybe he should examine that edict more closely on his side of things, she thought.

When he entered the office some time later, she almost forgot what she was doing. He looked as tired as she felt.

Did he have trouble sleeping at night?

"I didn't mean to fall asleep at lunch," she blurted out.

He shrugged and took off his hat, running his fingers through his hair. "Pregnant woman are tired all the time."

Of course he'd know; he'd had a pregnant wife at one time.

"I appreciate your letting me work later tonight to catch up."

"There's plenty to do, but it doesn't all have to be done between eight and five." He sat down and tilted back in his chair, gazing off at the wall opposite.

Dani didn't know if she should ask what the project was he wanted help on, or wait for him to bring it up. She expected a scathing remark about keeping up with the work or how those who sleep on the job don't stay employed.

Keeping watch surreptitiously, she waited for him to speak. It was some time before he brought his chair down on all four legs and looked at the messages stacked on his desk.

He still didn't tell her what he wanted to work on.

A little after six, he rose and crossed to the front of her desk, tossing a handful of messages there.

"Phone them in the morning for me. You ought to be able to handle everything. I'm going to call it a day." He turned and headed for the door.

"Wait!" She looked at the notes and then at him, puzzled. "Why did you want me to work late?"

He looked to the left, not quite meeting her eyes. "I was thinking you can adjust your hours if you wish. Take a longer lunch to get in a short nap."

Without waiting for her response, he opened the door and stepped into the twilight.

Dani was dumbfounded. For days he'd been harping that this was not the place for her. Yet when she'd given him cause to fire her, he'd worked around it.

She didn't understand the man at all.

But she was grateful for his change of heart.

Change of heart? Could there be more to his gesture than just her staying on the job?

Dare she even think of such a thing? Granted, she was lonely and yearned for companionship. But she was too wary to give her trust easily.

Connor had his own baggage to deal with. How would two such distrustful people ever find a common bond?

# Chapter Thirteen

The next two days passed without incident. Dani took two hours for lunch and napped, never sleeping as late as she had on Tuesday. Grateful for the consideration, she tried to thank Connor and was brushed off.

What did she expect? He was not going to win the Mr. Congeniality award.

On Friday Dani decided to work through lunch, to minimize the time she was away from her desk. It was half past twelve when Connor entered the office.

"What are you doing here? Isn't it lunch hour?"

Dani nodded, calmly continuing to work. "I'm working through lunch. I have a doctor's appointment this afternoon. Mick approved the switch."

"Are you sick?"

"No, routine checkup."

He nodded and went to his desk.

They worked in silence, though Dani was intensely aware of him. Every time he shifted, she glanced up. His hair was mussed from running his fingers through it. She'd seen him do it a dozen times, and could anticipate the action now.

He moved with an economy of motion. She'd love to just sit and gaze at the man, but carefully looked down lest he surprise her and catch her watching him.

"I could drive you in," he said.

"What?" She looked up. What was he talking about?

"I could drive you into Carson Creek this afternoon. I need to go pick up some things we ordered at the hardware store in town. I could drive you at the same time, if you don't mind going in the truck."

"I don't mind riding in the truck. But I can drive myself. There's no need to put you out."

Her heart skipped a beat. He was offering to drive her to and from Carson Creek? She remembered how tongue-tied she'd felt at lunch and on their picnic. To be enclosed in a truck for the trip would make her crazy.

Yet the thought was tantalizing, too. Maybe they could recapture a hint of the friendly atmosphere she'd found at the beginning of their dinner the other night.

Or maybe they'd end up arguing, as they usually did.

"You'll be tired, and it'll be dark by the time you drive back. I'd feel better if I was driving. There's no reason to take two vehicles, anyway. It's a waste of gas."

When he put it that way, it made sense.

Plus she'd feel better if someone else drove back after dark on that lonely road.

"Okay, then. Thanks."

"When's the appointment?"

"At four-thirty."

He rose and started for the door. "We'll leave at three forty-five. I'm going to get something to eat. Take your lunch hour. Doctor visits are covered."

He paused by the door and glanced back at her.

"Why don't you wear that pink dress? We might want to

grab a bite to eat in town, before heading home," he said, before he stepped outside.

Dani stared at the closed door in stunned surprise. Had he just asked her to dinner?

Promptly at three forty-five, Dani left her trailer and headed for the office. She'd dithered all afternoon about changing from jeans to a dress, as Connor had requested. Giving in, she hoped she wasn't making a fool of herself. But it was the least she could do, since he was driving her into town.

He was not at the office when she peeped in.

Mick looked up. "Connor said he'd be here in a minute. He had to check something out with one of the men. That storm looks as if it's moving in faster than we thought. I bet it rains before you get back."

"Good thing he's driving, then. I wouldn't relish tackling that road after dark in the rain."

"That truck of his will go through anything."

She heard its rumble out front and bade Mick goodbye. Starting down the stairs, she felt the butterflies in her stomach again. Connor stopped the vehicle at the bottom of the steps and climbed out.

She nodded calmly, hoping he didn't have a clue how nervous she felt. Every cell in her body seemed attuned to him. He'd changed into clean jeans and a new shirt. His shoulders looked wide, solid, dependable. His dark hair was combed, but she knew it wouldn't stay that way if he got frustrated and combed his fingers through it.

His eyes were hidden behind dark glasses. Maybe it was just as well. She swallowed hard and went to climb up into the truck's cab.

Once she was seated, he closed the passenger door and went

around to the driver's side. In only seconds they were off.

"Do you have a lot to pick up?" she asked, striving to calm her jangling nerves. The trip took forty minutes at best. Might as well start off with some polite conversation.

"If everything came in, the bed will be packed," he said glancing at her.

She waited, but he said nothing further. No comment about her dress, the order at the hardware store or anything else.

The minutes ticked by.

He cleared his throat. "You aren't expecting me to go in to the doctor's with you, are you?"

"Heavens no. You can drop me off. When I'm finished, I'll walk to the hardware store and meet you there."

For an instant, however, she wistfully wished someone would go with her. That there was someone to share the wonder of the experience and rejoice with her in the coming of her baby.

Once again she regretted the fact that she had no family. The birth of a baby deserved fanfare and celebration.

"I can wait in the truck," he said.

"No, I don't know how long I'll be. Carson Creek isn't that large. I can find the hardware store and have a nice walk to boot."

"Fine."

The next twelve miles passed in silence. Dani did her best to enjoy the scenery, though it still felt as if she were traveling through a green tunnel with the top blown off. The trees were thick and tall, shading the road.

She felt herself grow drowsy. She hadn't taken a nap at lunch today since she knew she'd be leaving work early. Now the soothing ride was having its effect. Maybe if she just rested her eyes for a couple of moments...

"Dani?"

Slowly she opened her eyes. Connor was leaning over her, shaking her shoulder gently.

"Wake up, we're here."

She blinked, then came wide-awake.

"Oh, I'm sorry, I didn't mean to fall asleep."

He made a wry face. "No harm done. Can't say my scintillating conversation kept you awake."

"What conversation? You're the strong silent type."

His eyes danced in amusement. "You think?"

She looked around at the low brick building that housed the medical offices. He didn't need to be so close. She was awake. He could sit back on his side of the truck and give her some breathing room.

Grabbing the door handle, she glanced at him. His face was only inches from her own. She could see herself reflected in his dark eyes, feel his breath skim across her cheeks.

Dani felt a curious sensation, as if she were floating. She couldn't look away. What would it be like to lean forward those scant few inches and brush her lips against his? To have him wrap her in his strong arms and kiss her like there was no tomorrow?

Yikes! She was hallucinating now. Kissing her was the last thing Connor had on his mind.

She scrambled to unfasten her seat belt as he leaned back in his seat.

"I'll meet you at the hardware store," she said, thrusting open the door and almost tumbling out of the truck. "I don't know how long I'll be. You'll still be there, right?" She glanced back, holding the door as a shield.

He nodded, looking somewhat puzzled.

Slamming the door, she turned and walked briskly up the short sidewalk leading to the medical offices.

Idiot! she berated herself. He'd think she was totally cuckoo. He'd done nothing but wake her up and her mind had spun the fantasy that sometimes came late at night.

She had to get a grip! Connor had given her a ride into town, nothing more.

Dani left the doctor's office happy with the report. She had gained a bit more weight than he'd wanted, but it was nothing to be concerned about. As she strolled down the street, she couldn't help smiling. The doctor had discussed planning for the actual birth. She had to decide soon if she wished to stay in Carson Creek or return to Denver. It wouldn't be too much longer before she held her darling baby girl or boy in her arms.

Her curiosity as to the gender of her child was strong, but she was determined to be surprised at the birth and had refused to let her obstetrician tell her.

She sidestepped around a couple in front of her, then stopped a moment, suddenly attentive to what was going on around her. The sidewalks were full of people. She'd had no idea there were this many people in Carson Creek.

"Excuse me, can you tell me how to get to the hardware store?" she asked a woman walking by.

"Jesse's place? Two more blocks down and then turn right on Summer Street. It's three blocks after the turn."

"Thank you. What's going on in town tonight?"

The woman looked at her in surprise. "Football, what else? We're playing Henley. The high school band and team will be marching through at six. Happens every time we have a home game with a big rival. Then everyone goes to the high school field to watch our team tromp the other."

Dani nodded her thanks and continued along the sidewalk, alert to the activity surrounding her. There was a preponderance of blue and gold—the school colors? Pennants waved. Excitement seemed to build as neighbors greeted each other and sought curbside spots to unfold lawn chairs.

Cars were no longer parked on the street. A sheriff's car cruised slowly along, the deputy calling greetings to folks from his open window.

Kids ran around and older folks gathered in small groups, chatting.

If she moved to Carson Creek, she and her child would become part of this. Maybe she'd have a son who'd want to play football. Maybe one day she'd be on the sidelines, proudly watching him march by on the way to a game with a rival high school.

Reaching Summer Street, she turned and immediately noticed the difference. It was practically deserted. She saw the sign for the hardware store and beneath it Connor's truck. The back was piled high, with a tarp covering everything. But she didn't see him.

Dani drew her coat closer, feeling the brisk wind as it blew across the parking lot. She headed for the glass double doors of the building. Connor came out just as she reached them.

"All set?" she asked brightly.

He nodded toward the truck. "Everything came in. It's still early to eat. Want to do something else first?"

"We could watch the parade," she suggested, curious about the customs of this small town.

"What parade?"

When she explained, he shrugged. "If you like. We'll leave the truck here and come back for it afterward."

Dani and Connor found a small niche on the main street that gave them a perfect view. Both sides were lined with people. The air was festive and laughter rang out from different groups.

Promptly at six they heard the beginning strains of a marching song. Dani leaned out to peer down the street, feeling excitement grow. She didn't know a soul in town except for Connor, but it didn't matter. She'd cheer the parade on with the best of them.

Another gust of wind had her shivering.

"You need a warmer coat," Connor said.

"I'll be fine for as long as the parade lasts, then we'll be inside."

He stepped closer, sheltering her from the wind. Another gust had her shivering again. This time he opened his own heavy jacket and drew her back against the warmth of his chest, wrapping the edges of the coat around her as far as they would reach.

Which wasn't far, but Dani felt blissfully warm and sheltered with Connor's hot body at her back. She looked over her shoulder and almost bumped noses with him.

"Thanks," she whispered.

"I can't have you freezing to death. Maybe this wasn't such a good idea."

Just then the band came into view. At least twenty teenagers were marching proudly, despite the wind and cold. Their uniforms were navy blue and white and gold, their hats worn at a jaunty angle.

The crowd cheered and clapped, Dani joining in.

"Know any of those kids?" Connor asked.

She shook her head. "No, but isn't it fun? Maybe some day I'll have a teenager marching in the band. Or playing football."

Connor was quiet, and a moment later Dani wondered if he was thinking about his own son. Would he have played ball? Marched in a band? Or gone into computers and science?

"If you want to leave, we can," she said.

Connor looked down at her in surprise.

"Why would I want to go? The parade isn't over yet."

"I thought it might make you remember your own son."

"Yeah, it does. But life goes on, Dani. I can't ever have Sammy with me again. He won't ever go to high school, play football or date. It's hard to accept sometimes, but I think I'm finally getting it. His life was short. It was great while he was here, but he's gone. I don't mind that these kids are doing their thing. The world can't stop because my son is no longer in it."

"Still, you don't have to watch."

"I'm okay."

Connor had his arms around her, holding her against his chest, trying to shelter her as best he could. She should have worn a heavier coat. And sturdier boots. He felt responsible. Why had he told her to wear a dress? She would have been warmer in her flannel shirt, jeans and boots.

She moved against him, straining to see everything, almost jumping up and down in glee watching the simple, hometown parade. Embracing life with all her enthusiasm.

Her movements were starting to cause serious problems. He held an armful of warm, delightful femininity.

And his long-starved body knew it.

For the first time since Catherine had died, he wanted a woman.

Not just any woman.

Dani.

The instant the thought flashed into his mind, a million

reasons why he shouldn't also crowded in. She worked for him. He didn't want to get embroiled with anyone. He suspected Dani was the type to feel deeply before she let herself become engaged in any liaison.

She trusted him. The irony ran deep. She trusted him, but could he trust himself?

The football team came into view, pretty cheerleaders leading the way. The boys raised arms above their heads, helmets concealing their faces. But the townsfolk knew their sons, and the cheers rose louder and louder.

A convertible followed, with coaches sitting up on the back, waving to the crowd.

Then it was over. The people began dispersing, most heading in the direction of the high school. In only a short time, Dani and Connor were back at the truck.

"That was such fun. Everyone seemed so excited for the team," she said, sitting back in her seat, fastening her seat belt. "I hope they win."

"A small town is like that. Everyone knows everyone else. And it'll be more fun for them to win on the home field."

"Denver was too impersonal. I think I'll stay here. Maybe I can get a job with the resort when it opens."

"Wait until you spend a winter here. You might change your mind," Connor warned. "Any place special where you want to eat?"

"No. The diner is fine."

"I thought about a place on the edge of town. It's an old farmhouse that's been converted to a restaurant."

He'd never been to it, but it would do justice to the dress she wore. And mean more than dinner at the diner.

He drew a quiet breath. Did he want it to mean more?

# Chapter Fourteen

The farmhouse restaurant was charming Dani thought as she gazed around when they entered. The entire ground floor of the old house had been converted to a dining area. Small tables with two and four chairs were scattered around the old parlor where the hostess seated them. The original fireplace was operational and a blazing fire heated the room.

They were seated near enough to the fire that they could enjoy it without becoming too hot. Dani quickly shed her jacket. The warmth was a welcome change from the bitter wind.

"This is lovely," she said as she gazed around. It was more elegant than anything she'd expected to find in Carson Creek. Or, truth be told, more elegant than she'd expected Connor to like. She glanced at him. He was staring at her.

"Do I have something on my face?" she asked.

He shook his head and reached for the menu.

She took her own menu and scanned the different selections, wondering about his look.

When they'd ordered, Dani smiled shyly. "Thanks for bringing me here. This is such a treat."

"It's just dinner."

"One I didn't have to fix for myself."

"I thought you liked to cook."

"I do, but not just for myself. Don't you get tired of cooking for one?"

"Mick comes over often enough."

"Tell me how you and Mick got involved in this project so far from home."

"Far from home?"

"Aren't you two from Fort Collins? That's at the other end of the state."

"We're from there. It's not home. I take my home with me."

*Now.*

The word wasn't said, yet it echoed in the silence.

"Okay then, home is here. How did you two go into partnership?"

Connor looked as if he didn't want to talk, but Dani didn't expect to sit in silence throughout the meal. And she was genuinely interested in learning more about Connor. And Mick, too, she reminded herself firmly.

Connor slowly began to tell her about their business dealings, and she hung on every word. Since she knew each of them, she could fill in the background beyond Connor's terse comments. She knew exactly who had done what in the various projects, even though he didn't explain. There was no need. She had a good grasp of each man's personality. Connor had more drive than Mick, but the older man balanced the partnership with experience and a definite patience in dealing with bureaucracy. It was interesting to gain a glimpse of their shared history.

Dani and Connor both chose prime rib. When the platters came, the amount of food was startling. Dani knew she would never finish even half. But it was so delicious she dug in with an appetite.

She tried to keep the conversation going, afraid to let silence swamp them. She was conscious of Connor on a level she'd never experienced before. He fascinated her. She knew the danger of that emotion. It led to wanting to know more about a person, which then led to thinking that there could be something between them.

Yet as a moth is drawn to the flame, she couldn't stop pushing to learn more. To give in to that desire to learn as much about him as she could. Curiosity, maybe. But compelling nonetheless.

She didn't understand why he'd invited her out for dinner, but she wasn't going to ask. She took the opportunity to gaze her fill, studying him when he wasn't looking, enthralled by the way the flickering firelight cast shadows on his face. She absorbed his deep voice, letting it seep through her like mulled wine. And she gathered every speck of knowledge he chose to share.

She was no closer to understanding the man when they left than she had been when they arrived. He'd sheltered her from the wind while watching the parade. But his conversation during dinner stayed on a superficial level. He rarely revealed much of his own feelings and hopes.

Yet he had shown her a tender side she doubted few had seen.

It was pouring rain when they stepped from the restaurant onto the old-fashioned porch.

"Oh my gosh, this is awful!" Dani exclaimed when a gust of wind blew a blast of rain on them both, even beneath the shelter of the porch roof. She was relieved he'd be the one to drive home in the downpour. What if she'd driven herself into town that afternoon?

"I'll bring the truck close. Wait until I come to get you so you don't slip on the walkway." Connor instructed, hurrying toward the truck, not waiting for her response.

For a moment Dani's independent streak reared up. She didn't like taking orders any more than the next person. Then common sense took hold. Of course she'd wait. She wouldn't risk harm to herself or her baby.

Once again a tendril of warmth sparked deep inside, that someone else cared for what happened to her—even if it was just getting safely to the truck.

The ride home seemed treacherous to Dani. The low spots in the gravel road had already filled with water. The rain beat hard on the windshield, the wipers ineffective in clearing the deluge. The trees on either side of the road swayed and bent in the onslaught, making it seem as if they would come crashing down on the truck. She shivered, feeling sorry for the kids playing football in this downpour. Or would they have called off the game due to the weather?

"I never could have made it myself," she murmured after the truck splashed through another deep puddle. The wind gusted again, shuddering against the vehicle.

"It's pretty bad, but it could be worse. It could be snow. The county plans to pave the road but they wanted all the heavy equipment gone so their weight wouldn't damage the road once it's built," Connor said. He seemed perfectly at ease maneuvering his truck through the storm. Swerving to avoid a fallen branch, he threw her a quick look.

Dani could see him faintly in the illumination from the dashboard. Otherwise the darkness was complete except for the headlights slashing through the rain, swallowed by the night.

She tried to relax. If he wasn't worried, she wouldn't worry, either. She trusted Connor completely.

Blinking, she gazed out into the tempest.

*She trusted him?*

She'd sworn off trusting men.

Of course, trusting him to drive them home safely wasn't the same as trusting a man with her heart and future. That wasn't in the cards, no matter how much she sometimes wistfully wished it were.

But if she ever dared risk forming an attachment again, Connor would be the one she'd trust to do what he said and stay the course. Look at his continued devotion to his family, gone three years now.

Would he ever consider starting a new family? Finding a new love? Or was he like her, too hurt and battered by life to venture forth again?

It was late by the time they reached the construction site. The thick gravel on the road and access area was dotted with puddles. Branches and limbs from trees had blown down. Some skipped across the open area, driven by the wind. Mud was everywhere else.

Connor drove the truck right to her trailer. "I hope this eases soon. The forecast said it'd blow over by Sunday. I'm counting on it."

"So there'll be no problem working on Monday?"

"Let's hope not. Wait there, I'll come around to help you in."

She took her key from her purse, to have in hand. When he opened the door, the wind blew through the truck, strong and cold. Dani shivered and stepped out into the rain. They almost ran to her steps. She had the door open in no time.

"Want to come in for coffee or something?" Dani asked,

rushing inside and turning to hold the door. The trailer felt blessedly warm after their mad dash through the icy rain.

Connor hesitated a moment, then nodded and stepped inside.

She'd invited him to be polite. She hadn't really expected him to take her up on the offer.

Now what? After watching him throughout dinner, Dani had grown more and more aware of him and the long-dormant needs of her own body. It had become more difficult by the minute to remember her vow of non-involvement. A sweet kiss. A brush of his hand. She fantasized about more.

She hung up their jackets and went to the kitchenette to prepare the coffee. She busied herself with grinding coffee beans, putting on the kettle, wondering what she had to go with coffee. Some cookies, maybe? The brownies were long gone.

She was stalling and she knew it.

Maybe he'd gulp the hot beverage down when she gave it to him and dash away.

Connor sat on the sofa, looking at home in the small trailer, at ease. She could see him easily from the kitchenette. And she envied him. Her nerves were dancing in anticipation. The blood pounded through her veins. The low light set a romantic tone. She frowned. Surely he didn't think she'd set the stage for something more than coffee and good-night.

Dani found a package of cookies, opened it and placed a few on a plate, wishing she had made more brownies recently. Connor loved them.

Wasn't that old saying the way to a man's heart was through his stomach?

She kept her gaze on the teakettle, willing it to boil. She was *not* trying to get to Connor's heart. It was simply that, as a cook, she appreciated it when someone liked what she'd made.

When the coffee was ready, she made tea for herself and took their mugs and the plate of cookies to the living room.

"Looks good," he said, rising as she entered, and reaching for the mugs. He placed them on the end table and waited until she sat in the flanking chair before resuming his seat.

"Tomorrow is Mick's birthday, did you know?" he asked.

"No, I didn't. I wish you'd said something earlier, I could have bought a gift in Carson Creek."

"He doesn't want gifts. But the men and I planned a sort of party."

"What's a 'sort of' party?"

"It's a party—but no alcohol. We're holding it here at the site, which looks like it'll be a good thing if this rain keeps up. We've enclosed one section of the main building. If the rain hasn't leaked through, we'll hold it there. You're invited—if you want to come. A few of the guys will bring a girlfriend. Some of the wives who come down periodically will be there, so you won't be the only woman."

She started to ask if that would be considered fraternizing with the other workers, but wisely kept quiet. He'd invited her. That was enough.

"I'd like to come. What time?"

"Seven."

Connor took a handful of cookies and slowly ate them.

Dani contented herself with watching him and sipping the herbal tea she'd prepared. It was cozy in the warm trailer with the rain beating down on the metal roof. The wind gusted from time to time, shaking the trailer slightly, but she wasn't concerned. She was pleasantly tired after the long day. Even her jangled nerves were soothed.

It was quiet evenings like this she'd hoped to have once she married. Would Marc ever have settled for such evenings?

"Have you thought of a name for your baby?" Connor asked.

"Not yet. I keep trying different ones out. Some sound great when a person is an adult, but too formal for a baby. Yet I don't want him or her to have a childish name when grown. Did you and Catherine know right away what you wanted to name Sammy?"

"He was named for both our fathers, actually. My father is Samuel Norris, Catherine's dad is George Samuel Andrews."

"And what did you pick for a girl?"

"She wanted Brittany. I wanted Heather."

"They're both pretty. I like Melanie. I guess I'll have to decide before long."

Dani sipped her tea. It would be fun to name a baby for a family member, to carry on tradition through the generations. Only she didn't care to carry on the tradition her own parents had left her.

"It's getting late. I should go," Connor said, setting down his empty coffee cup.

"Thanks again for dinner and driving me in to begin with. I would have ended up staying overnight in Carson Creek rather than face that trip back by myself," Dani said.

She fetched his heavy jacket and handed it to him, remembering how warm it had felt wrapped partway around her earlier when they'd watched the parade.

"I enjoyed tonight," she said softly.

He started to speak, but instead swept her into his arms and kissed her.

Dani was startled, then forgot everything except the

delightful sensations that splashed through her body. His hold was firm, pulling her to his long length, molding her against the hard play of his muscles. She could scarcely breathe, but who needed air when pulsating pleasure pounded through her veins? Her own arms wrapped around his neck and she responded to the kiss with a hunger that had been building for days.

She felt totally enveloped. His warmth invaded and heated her blood. His kiss deepened. Her own response matched his. She couldn't believe this was happening. Did thinking a thing make it come true?

It was as if he was as hungry as she for touch and feeling and connection. Did he miss contact with others as she did? Or was this more—special, meant for her alone?

He stopped suddenly, pulling back.

She wanted to hold on, to clutch him close and never let go, but slowly she released her hold around his neck. She gazed up at him. It was his move. What next?

"I shouldn't have done that," he said, his gaze roaming over her face.

His thumb came up to slowly brush across her lips. Lips slightly swollen and damp from their kiss.

She almost cried when he touched her so gently. And heard the apology in his tone. She didn't want an apology. She wanted another soul-searing kiss.

"Please don't say you're sorry," she whispered. Why couldn't he have enjoyed it as much as she? Why not want another? They were young, healthy, and not attached to another living soul.

He looked at her, his expression fierce. "I shouldn't be kissing anyone."

Dani stood on tiptoe and brushed her lips against his, wishing she could do more. If he wouldn't kiss her, she'd kiss him.

With a short farewell, Connor spun around and left. The trailer almost rocked from the slamming of the door.

Dani hugged herself, feeling chilled to the bone with his abrupt departure.

Neither was attached to another living soul, but Connor hadn't let go of one who was dead. Was that why he'd left so abruptly?

# Chapter Fifteen

Connor stood on the trailer steps, tilting his head back, facing the rain. The cold drops soaked his hair and face. His jacket absorbed the moisture at an astonishing rate, and would be soaked through before long.

He hoped the cold would bring him to his senses. The wind blew icy blasts down his neck. Slowly he drew in a deep breath.

What had he done?

Given in to temptation without a thought to anything but his burning need to hold Dani, to feel her against him, to taste her mouth and see if the undercurrent of sexual tension was mutual.

And if her response was anything to go by, it was.

He was a fool. Stepping down, he walked to his truck, ignoring the rain, ignoring the puddles he splashed through. He had no business kissing anyone.

What about Catherine?

*Catherine's gone.*

He groaned softly, opening the truck door and sliding in behind the wheel. He knew she was gone. Had known it every day for the three years she'd been dead.

*Time to move on.*

He clenched his fists and pounded the steering wheel. He

had moved on. He had fashioned a life for himself away from all he knew and loved. He pushed Catherine and Sammy to the back of his mind during the day.

But at night, they were there—just out of reach.

He could close his eyes and see them. Doing so now, he frowned. There was nothing there.

Then the image of Dani's dancing curls appeared. Her smile. Her feisty determination when she argued with him. Her laughter when Mick told a joke. Her blue eyes bright with expectation and anticipation.

Connor snapped open his eyes and started the truck. He had to get home. See the photo of Catherine, recapture her image in his mind.

He couldn't forget Catherine and Sammy. And he'd never forget the endless days and nights of pain and loneliness when they'd first been gone. His life as he'd known it had ended. It had taken him months to get back on an even keel, to function like a normal person.

He couldn't go through something like that again, no matter how tempted he might be to kiss Dani, to spend time with her.

Even if he were to give in, she deserved better. After the father of her baby had deserted her, she deserved to have a man who would love her and that baby when it came. Who would stand by her through thick and thin. Not a burned-out guy who would be moving on once this project was completed.

He walked into his trailer and flicked on the light. It was cold. Sterile. Except for the picture of Catherine and Sammy, nothing personal was on display.

Connor contrasted it to the warmth of Dani's trailer. He couldn't remember any personal items, but there was something about her place that cried home. His was just shelter from the storm.

He picked up the photo and stared down at the two people he'd loved most in the world. Catherine looked so happy. She had always been happy. At least he had that to hold on to. And Sammy... How proud he'd been, going to school just like a big kid. He would have been eight now, in third grade. Connor and Catherine had discussed getting Sammy a dog when he was older. Eight would have been a great age to have a dog.

As Connor stared into the beloved faces, he felt an easing of the tension, a fading of the old ache. They'd been a part of his life and he would always have the memories. But they were gone.

*Time to move on.*

He traced his fingers over Catherine's cheeks. Cold glass met his touch. He touched Sammy's nose. Only cold glass. With a sigh, Connor carried the photograph into the bedroom and put it in the top drawer. It was time to move on.


Dani loved Saturdays best, she thought, snuggled down in her bed. She could sleep in as late as she wanted. Do a few chores, then take a nap if she wished. Eat when she wanted, and wear comfortable clothes.

So why did she awaken at six forty-five, her mind spinning with images of Connor? She had to find some technique that would enable her to forget him!

Forget that kiss.

Might as well tell her to forget to eat. She doubted she'd ever forget that kiss. It was unlike any she'd ever received. He was unlike anyone she'd ever known.

And definitely off-limits.

Stay away from him, she told herself, trying to fall back

asleep.

Memories ended and imagination took hold. As she was drifting off, she could see Connor forging a path through a crowded room, sweeping her away to a dark corner, kissing her until she couldn't remember her name. Or whisking her to a sunlit hillside, where the two of them would be alone on a carpet of wildflowers.

It was late morning when Dani woke again. She refused to dwell on daydreams and set to work cleaning the trailer and baking cookies to give to Mick at the party. At least she could contribute something.

# Chapter Sixteen

Just before seven that evening, Dani was ready. She wore her yellow dress and had done her best with her hair and makeup. She looked good, she thought, smiling at herself in the mirror. The sparkle in her eye was from the thought of the party, she told herself. The color in her cheeks came from the short walk she'd taken that afternoon after the rain had stopped.

The knock on the door surprised her. She quickly went to answer it. Bill Frates stood on the steps.

"Hi, Dani. I thought I'd walk you over to the party. It's still muddy in spots."

"Why, thank you, Bill. I appreciate that." She put on her heavy coat, gathered the cookies and was ready.

The enclosed area of the new resort was huge. Two industrial-size heaters were doing their best to warm the place up, but since tarps comprised a portion of the walls, it was a never-ending challenge. Still, she was surprised at how warm it was. Enough to take off her coat. She left it in the pile near the door.

Almost everyone who worked on the site was present, Dani noted, plus a dozen or so wives and girlfriends. She spotted Mick right away and headed over to greet him and give him the cookies she'd baked.

A three-piece band was at one end of the room, warming up. The plywood flooring would provide ample space for dancing. Dani recognized one of the band members—Moose, the guy who ran the crane. Obviously the group was comprised of construction workers who liked to play.

"Dani, glad you came," Mick greeted her with a big smile.

She held out the bag of cookies. "Happy Birthday, Mick."

"What's this?"

"You said you liked oatmeal cookies, so I made you a batch."

"They're my favorite! Thank you!" He leaned over and kissed her on the cheek. "There's lots of food on the table over there. And drinks are at the makeshift bar. Help yourself."

A young couple came to wish Mick happy birthday and Dani drifted away, not wanting to be drawn into the conversation. She studied the skeleton of the building, noting the window openings where tarps held back the cold. The high ceilings with their exposed duct work and conduits would be enclosed by the end of construction season.

What would this space be when the resort was complete? A ballroom? A convention hall?

She ambled around, smiling at those men she recognized, nodding politely to others who greeted her. Two stopped to introduce her to their wives.

The music was wild and fast. Couples danced, men breaking in and switching partners. Everyone seemed to be having a great time. Dani strayed to the sidelines, near one of the heaters, enjoying the music and wistfully watching the people dancing. Her carefree days were nearly gone. In only a couple of months she'd be a mother. She'd have to stay home and care for her baby for a long time. Who knew when she'd attend another dance?

"Care to dance?" One of the younger men came up to her, already puffing slightly from exertion.

"Maybe later," Dani said with a smile. Mindful of Connor's first prediction, she had no plans to dance, but didn't want to get into a discussion. It was enough to smile and gently refuse.

"Sure." He grinned and headed off to find another partner.

Dani looked around. Had Connor not come, after all? Suddenly she spotted him talking with a group of men across the room. He glanced up then—directly at Dani.

She felt a flush of heat and quickly looked away. She didn't want him to think she was looking for him.

Maybe she'd get something to eat and then leave. She walked to the buffet table and selected a few pieces of finger food. Nibbling, she wandered to where one of the men was holding forth as if he were a bartender. She watched for a moment, laughing at his nonsense, then ordered up the house specialty—Windhaven Windy—a mixture of cola and his special secret ingredient. Sipping it, Dani thought the secret ingredient was lemonade. It was not the best drink she'd ever had.

Reclaiming her spot near the heater, she had scarcely taken another bite of her food when Connor materialized.

"Dance?"

She looked up and her heart skipped a beat. "I don't think so. Too fast for me."

Then the melody registered. It was a slow, dreamy song, quite different from the fast-stepping rhythms that had been playing all evening.

"You can handle this." He took her plate and put it on the floor. Holding out his hand, he stood there, waiting.

Dani took a deep breath and stretched out her own hand.

When his closed over hers, she let her breath go. The magic she always experienced around Connor invaded.

Trying to ignore the clamoring desire, she walked calmly to the cleared area and moved into his arms. She would not dwell on the memory of their kiss. This was a sedate, staid dance in front of the entire work crew. A duty dance.

A pang struck.

Was it only a duty dance?

"Having a good time?" Connor asked.

She nodded, her gaze firmly fixed to the left of his shoulder.

"Speak to Mick?"

She nodded.

"Are you not speaking to me?"

With that she looked up and saw amusement dancing in his dark eyes.

"Sure. What shall I say?"

"Invite me in for coffee when this is over and we'll see what we can discover to talk about."

"Talk? Or something else?"

"Now, Miss Dani Winthrop, what else could we do?"

She bit her lower lip, trying to keep from grinning in delight. "I might make some brownies. I know you like them."

"I liked dessert last night, too," he said, drawing her even closer as they moved to the music.

She admitted to being slightly surprised to find out what a great dancer Connor was. She'd thought that, with him being stuck at construction sites most of the time, his social amenities would be in short supply. He danced better than anyone she'd ever danced with. They seemed in perfect synchronization, floating to the melody, in tune with the music and each other.

It was only a dance. She had to remind herself more and

more frequently lately that nothing could come of a relationship between Connor and her.

But for a moment, just the tiniest moment, she wished something wonderful could develop. Wished they were two different people who could meet, fall in love and trust that the future would be perfect.

Instead, she was afraid to trust again. Wary of commitment by others. What would it be like to walk through life unafraid?

Connor continued to stand beside her when the music stopped. Several of the men gave them curious looks, but he seemed to be unaware.

"Want something to drink?" he asked after a moment.

"Not the Windhaven Windy," she said firmly.

He looked puzzled.

"Tonight's bartender is coming up with wild concoctions instead of giving out plain sodas, and that was one. It was gross."

"I'll avoid that. I'll make sure he gives us plain cola, if that's what you want."

"Or we could have coffee at my place," she said daringly.

When he didn't respond immediately, Dani wanted to sink through the floor. He'd suggested it earlier, but hadn't he meant it? Was he worried she planned to seduce him?

She looked away, afraid she'd burst out laughing. It was too ludicrous for words. She was almost seven months pregnant with another man's baby. Would anyone in his or her right mind think she could seduce a man at this stage? Especially someone like Connor?

"I should stay a bit longer. It's Mick's night and I don't want to cut out early," Connor said slowly.

"I understand." Dani tried to keep her tone offhand and

casual. She could feel the sting of embarrassed color in her cheeks. How soon before she could slip away and hide in her trailer?

"I think I'd like something cold to drink, after all. I can get it."

She smiled brightly and started for the makeshift bar. Anything to get away from the situation. Once out of sight, she'd make a dash for her trailer and stay there until Monday morning!

"I'll get it. You wait here." Connor touched her lightly on the shoulder and headed for the crowd around the bar. Dani debated dashing away the minute his back was turned, but knew that would give rise to speculation she didn't want.

She wished she hadn't so impetuously invited him to her trailer. He'd probably just been making small talk. In the future, she'd make sure she kept her distance. Connor was her boss, nothing more.

When she saw him heading back, panic flared. Bill Frates joined her before Connor reached her. Bill had invited her to join him for dinner several times. Dani had always refused, but she tried to remain on friendly terms with him. And he obviously held no hard feelings. He'd escorted her to the dance to make sure she made it without mishap.

"Care to dance?" he asked.

Before she could frame a polite refusal, Connor arrived and held out the cola. "She's sitting this one out."

Bill looked puzzled.

"With me," Connor said firmly.

"Oh, sure, boss. Maybe later."

Bill looked at each of them speculatively, then turned and strolled away.

Dani sipped the cold beverage, glad to have something to do to cover her surprise. Connor would give rise to rampant speculation if he continued acting like that. One would almost think his tone was possessive.

"This is nice," she said, casting around for a neutral topic of conversation. "Do you have parties often? Seems a good way for everyone to let off some steam."

"There'll be a big bash at the end of the season. Not all of the men will return next spring. Some will find other jobs during the winter. Others do winter work, like snow plowing, or working the ski resorts, and are ready to return to construction when the weather turns good. This party is an exception—for Mick's birthday."

The man of honor joined them just then and the three chatted as they watched the activities.

When Dani thought a sufficient time had elapsed, she excused herself, claiming to need the ladies' room. Instead, she headed for the coats and dug hers out. With a wistful glance behind her at the festivities, she let herself out into the cold night.

She carefully made her way to her trailer. The mud was frozen in spots, still soft in others. The wind had died, and the chilly air was still. She wished she'd brought a flashlight, but she reached the trailer without mishap.

Inside, it was warm and cozy and quiet. Too quiet. She could still hear the music from the party.

She slipped off her shoes and prepared a pot of tea. She'd read for a little while, then go to bed. Tomorrow she could sleep in late and maybe take a walk along the lake, if the ground had dried up enough.

The baby must have liked the party, she thought a few

minutes later as she settled on the sofa to begin to read a mystery she'd brought with her. Her child was actively moving around. Dani wondered if it could also hear the music and was dancing.

A knock on the door startled her. Peering through the peephole, she saw Connor. Dani opened the door.

"I came for that coffee," he said.

She stood aside, butterflies dancing in her stomach. He'd come for coffee, but was that all?

Quickly she switched on more lights.

"Have a seat. I boiled water for tea just a few minutes ago, so it won't take long to reheat for coffee. I thought you wanted to stay at the party longer."

"I did. But I want to see you more. Why did you leave?"

"Oh." Dani didn't know what to say. "It was time."

He shrugged out of his jacket and flung it over the back of a chair. "Coffee?" he said when she seemed glued to the spot.

Flustered, she turned toward the kitchenette. But Connor stopped her, his hand on her shoulder. She turned slowly and looked up into his eyes.

"Dani," he said slowly. Then he lowered his mouth to hers.

The bright lights should have dampened the mood. But nothing could dim the excitement of his embrace. Before she knew it, he'd wrapped her in his arms and deepened the kiss. His lips were cool from the night air. He tasted of cola and Connor. His arms held her strongly, yet with a hint of tender emotion.

Wrapping her arms around him, she gave herself to the kiss. *Never question good fortune* was her last coherent thought.

He felt solid and hot and strong. The little zings of energy surging through her were delightful. She felt free and alive and brimming with passionate energy.

His heartbeat matched hers. Time seemed to stop then. Eternity was in his kiss.

He took a step nearer the door and fumbled for the light switch, flicking it off, leaving only the lamp by the table to provide illumination.

It was romantic, she thought fuzzily through the roiling sensations. The faint, distant music lent a fey quality to the night. They were alone in the world, just the two of them. In seconds all thought fled. Dani was consumed by the fierce desire that raged through her. Consumed by the feelings and sensations she floated on.

Only Connor had ever elicited such a response from her. Was the man magic?

Or just very, very special?

They were dancing. She knew it as they moved across the room. Slowly, to some rhythm she could only hear in her mind. It was slow, sensuous, romantic. Wrapped in a world of two, Dani wished the night would never end.

She was floating. It was magical!

The pounding on the door was starling.

"What the heck?" Connor glared at the door. The hammering was relentless.

"Should I see who it is?" she whispered, standing.

" I'll check it out."

He swiftly crossed to the door, running his fingers through his hair. If he thought to bring order, Dani mused, he'd missed the mark.

Connor flung open the door. One of the workmen stood there, fist raised to knock again.

"Boss, there's trouble. Mick's trying to handle it, but sent me for you. It's Moose. He's fighting with Bob and they're really going at it."

Connor nodded, already reaching for his jacket. "I'll be right there."

He looked at her. "I have to go."

She nodded.

"I'll be back."

Dani said nothing, too conscious of the man watching them. Connor waited a moment, then stepped outside, pulling the door shut behind him.

She crossed the room slowly, pushing the dead bolt home with a click. She was still breathing hard from their kisses. And her blood felt inflamed, warming every inch of her. She hoped he could stop the fight without getting involved.

Rational thought began to seep in. She at least had held an illusion with Marc that there was a chance for happy ever after. She had none of that with Connor. Dare she hope his feelings for her would grow? Or was he just passing time until they wrapped up for the winter.

She suspected walking away from Connor would be far worse than when Marc had ended their relationship.

She knew herself. She was already feeling more for Connor than was safe. Where was her lofty determination to stay clear of any association? Of all people to become entangled with—a man still in love with his late wife!

Dani turned off the light and went to get ready for bed. She really hoped Connor didn't return. But if he did, she wouldn't open the door to temptation again.

# Chapter Seventeen

By the time Connor and Mick had settled things and sent everyone home, it was late. Connor walked with his partner to the trailers. Without conscious thought, he looked at Dani's. It sat in total darkness.

Not that he blamed her. He frowned. Show some finesse, he admonished himself. She'd invited him in for coffee, and he'd jumped her as soon as the door was closed.

"Until that fracas, it was a good party," Mick said as they drew near Connor's trailer.

"For most of us. Moose will regret it come Monday when I tell him I'm docking his pay for the damages."

"They weren't that extensive."

"I should fire him for bringing liquor. He knows the rule."

"If it happened any other time, I'd go along with you. But tonight was a party and some guys can't party without booze."

"Then he should have gone into town and found some action there."

"Speaking of action, I saw you and Dani dancing," Mick said.

"So?" Connor grew tense. Was Mick going to make some ribald comment? If he said anything about Dani—

"Just it was nice to see. She's lonely, I think. She doesn't have any family, you know."

"I heard."

"I don't think she knows what she's going to do when the baby comes. She even talked about settling down around here."

"She told me that."

"Ah. Well, then. Good night." Mick kept on walking toward his trailer. Connor watched until the older man entered.

"What was that all about?" he asked softly. Mick wasn't trying matchmaking, was he? If he were, the last thing Connor wanted him to know was what had gone on in Dani's trailer that night.

He entered his own, flipping on the lights. Once again it struck him as sterile and cold. He looked toward Catherine's picture, then remembered he'd moved it. Not even that remained for decoration.

Catherine would have had the place fixed up, made it homey.

Catherine. He missed her.

Kissing Dani had been dumb. Their relationship would never amount to anything. Surely she knew that. She wasn't weaving fantasies of happy ever after, was she? Not after a couple of kisses.

He had a resort to build. And other projects to monitor. Maybe he'd take a trip up to their site in Pueblo and see how the foreman was running things. The weekly updates via fax might not be covering everything.

It was an excuse to leave, Connor acknowledged as he headed for bed. Putting several hundred miles between himself and Dani Winthrop seemed wise at the moment. And once he returned, it would be business as usual—emphasis on the business part.

He had no intention of kissing his secretary again.

Despite the sunshine on Sunday, it remained cold. Dani ventured forth for a short walk along the lake, but was glad to return home. She made headway on her mystery novel, but found her mind wandering from time to time, wondering where Connor was and if he'd returned last night. Had he tried the door even though the lights were out? Or seen the darkened trailer and not bothered?

From time to time she glanced out the window. If she saw him, she could…what? Invite him in for coffee?

Feeling restless after lunch Dani began baking. So what if it was brownies. If she liked to make brownies, she would. Maybe Mick would like some.

As if thinking about the older man conjured him up, he knocked on the door.

"Come in," Dani said, hiding her disappointment that it wasn't the other partner. "You're just in time. I've made some brownies. They're baking now and will be ready soon."

"Smells real good. I came to see how you were doing. I didn't see you go for a walk today."

"I went early, but didn't stay long. It's too cold."

"Yeah, that storm dumped a lot of rain, but it was ahead of the cold front or it would have been snow. Another storm is due in later this week. I think our days here are becoming numbered."

"Did you enjoy your party?" Dani asked, fixing them each something hot to drink—herbal tea for her, coffee for Mick.

"Until Moose and the boys started fighting. I didn't get a chance to dance with the prettiest girl there, however. Connor beat me to it."

"Oh?" She would not be jealous. It didn't matter to her who Connor danced with.

"You, I mean." Mick smiled and winked.

"Hardly the prettiest one there."

Dani felt flattered that the older man took the effort to make her feel special.

She cleared her throat and tried to sound nonchalant. "Where's Connor today? Not working, I hope."

Mick looked at her sharply. So much for sounding casual.

"He left this morning for Pueblo. He'll be back later in the week."

"Pueblo?"

"We have a small shopping center going up there. We have a foreman running the job. He reports in weekly, but Connor got some bee in his bonnet about wanting to check it out in person. If we can't trust Mick after all these years, we might as well hang it up. Did you enjoy the party?"

They talked about the party and the storm and the accelerated schedule Mick and Connor planned to implement because of the last storm and ones already predicted.

But always in the back of her mind was the question of why Connor had left. He'd made no mention of a trip during the previous week. Or even Saturday night.

The next week seemed to drag slowly by. Dani entered the office each day half expecting, half hoping to see Connor stride in, his hair tousled from running his fingers through it, his eyes taking in everything, their dark depth giving away little in return.

Instead, his desk remained conspicuously empty.

Mick handled the office questions, decisions and planning. He also spent a lot of time out with the men. The entire camp seemed focused on working longer hours, to get as much done as they could before buttoning up for the winter.

Dani knew enough to run her part efficiently. With her naps at lunch, the days fell into a routine that was easily manageable. The nights were a little lonely, but she was used to those. As long as she kept her fantasies firmly in check, she was fine.

On Wednesday Connor phoned. Dani took the call.

"Is Mick there?" he asked. No hello for her.

"He's out on the site. Should I try to find him?"

"No, tell him to give me a call when he comes in."

"Are things going okay there?" she asked.

"Fine."

She waited, but he obviously wasn't going to say more.

"Things are going fine here, too," Dani said. Couldn't she think of anything else to say?

"Good. Have Mick call." He hung up.

Slowly she replaced the receiver. What had she expected? More than that brisk phone call, obviously.

She jotted the message for Mick and tried not to feel hurt that Connor had been so abrupt.

By Friday, the entire camp was talking about the impending storm. The weather had warmed up during the week, so snow wasn't a threat, but major precipitation and high winds were predicted.

"At least it'll strike on the weekend again," Dani said to Mick late Friday afternoon. The trees were already swaying in the wind. The sky churned with dark clouds.

"By Monday it'll probably blow over, and everyone can get back to work," she said optimistically.

"I don't know, this one might last a few days. It's a slow-moving storm and has already caused minor flooding in

Wyoming and the northern part of the state."

"Will the lake water rise?" Dani had an instant picture of the entire site being engulfed.

"Not so we'd notice. I'm more concerned with the winds. We're battening down the hatches today, to make sure damage is minimal. But I wouldn't be surprised if we have some damage because of the high wind."

"Isn't there anything else to do?"

Mick shook his head. "We've built it as strong as we can. This'll be a good test. Anything that doesn't hold up can be replaced."

The wind came before the rain. Dani was buffeted by it as she walked to her trailer after work. Gusting, it swirled leaves and small twigs around. She was grateful for last week's rain, which kept the dust down.

By the time she heated her supper, the rain had started, the drops sounding like hail against the metal roof of the trailer. The wind battered the sides, rocking the trailer slightly. She shivered after one fierce gust, grateful to be inside, warm and safe.

Going to bed later, she found the storm was not conducive to sleep. From time to time she heard a sharp crack as a branch fell from a tree, startling her. She stared into the darkness, straining her eyes to see outside. Except for a few pools of light from other trailers, the storm clouds obliterated everything.

Lying awake, she grew restless. Maybe she should try reading her book. She was close to the end and wanted to see if her guess about who the villain was would prove correct.

She rose and went to the living room to find the book. The light from the hall was all she needed.

Just then a loud crack sounded, as if it were right on top of her. The entire trailer shook, then cold air swooped in and enveloped her.

Dani ran back to the bedroom, stopping in the doorway in horror. A tree had smashed across the end of her trailer, ripping a gash in the roof and side. Rain swirled in, cold and wet. Her bed was covered in branches and pine needles.

She grabbed her bathrobe from the nearby chair and put it on. Fumbling for her sneakers, she got them on, too. All warmth had fled. Rain was soaking the carpet, blowing onto the bed. The light was off, but illumination from the hall enabled her to determine the damage. It looked as if the entire back corner of the trailer had been crushed.

There was no way she could spend the night in the room. Rain would have everything sopping wet in minutes. And she wouldn't trust the tree not to shift and settle even more.

She started for the living room and then reconsidered. With a wary eye on the tree, she got a clean pair of jeans and a couple of shirts, then hurried from the bedroom. Dressing quickly, she went to assess the damage one more time. The rain, driven by the wind, hadn't abated. Everything was soaked. The blow had shattered the windows. Pieces of tree limbs, bent metal and glass dusted the floor, the bed, the dresser.

She put on her heavy jacket. Forget about an umbrella; it wouldn't stand a chance in the wind. She wished there was cell service. She hated to go out into the rain, but needed help.

Hurrying through the mud and rain, she banged on the door to Mick's trailer. He opened it seconds later. When he recognized her, he practically pulled her into the trailer.

"Dani, what's wrong? What in the world are you doing out in this storm? You're not having the baby, are you?"

Dani shook her head, grateful for the warmth.

"No. A tree crashed through my bedroom. There's a huge

hole in the ceiling and wall, and rain is pouring in. I can't stay there. It's freezing in the trailer."

"You're not hurt, are you?" His concern was immediate.

"No, I was in the living room when it hit. Thankfully. There are two branches on the bed right where I would have been." She shivered, aware for the first time how close she'd come to possibly being injured. Or worse.

"Stay here, I'll get dressed and see what I can do."

"I'm not sure anyone can do anything tonight. Everything's getting wet. It's pouring out there."

In the short time it had taken her to run from her place to his, her hair had been drenched and the shoulders of her jacket soaked.

"Take off your jacket. I'll bring you a sweatshirt from my room. And a towel for your hair."

Mick came from his bedroom a few moments later, fully dressed and wearing a yellow slicker. He handed her a large sweatshirt and hand towel. Dani gratefully pulled on the first and then began to dry her hair.

"You wait here. I'll be back after I assess the damage," he said, heading for the door.

She nodded, glad to comply. The storm was frightening enough without having to go out in it again.

By the time Dani had her hair mostly dry and had warmed up, Mick returned, Bob and Tommy with him.

"We've managed to cover the things in your bedroom with tarps, and tie them down. What's wet will have to dry out when the rain stops. We closed the bedroom door, so the rest of the place will stay dry. We need to cut away the tree before we can assess the damage fully. Can't do that until morning at the earliest."

"Do you think any more trees will fall?" She felt vulnerable. What if a tree fell right across the living room when she was sleeping?

Another sharp crack sounded. A moment later the ground shook slightly as another tall tree fell. Tommy popped outside with his flashlight. He returned a moment later. "Couldn't see anything. Must have been farther away than it sounded. Some of the other men are out. One of the campers near the lake got hit by falling branches."

"Do you have what you need for the night?" Mick asked.

Dani looked surprised. "Shouldn't I return home?"

"I'd feel better if you'd spend the rest of the night here. You can have my bed. I'll catch some sleep on the sofa if I get a chance. First, I'm going back out to see what else has been damaged. Your place won't hold the heat, anyway, with that gash. No sense wasting propane trying."

"I can't take your bed," she protested. "I can use the sofa."

"I'll be out for a while, honey. You get some rest. Fresh sheets are in the small closet by the bathroom."

Mick and the others left. Dani made up the bed with fresh linens and gratefully climbed into it. She took off her shoes and jeans, keeping everything else on. She was still a bit cold and the sweatshirt felt good. In seconds, she drifted to sleep.

It was a troubled rest, however, for she was jarred awake every time she heard a limb break or the wind rocked the trailer.

She awoke near dawn to use the bathroom. Peeking into the living room afterward, she saw Mick fast asleep on the sofa. The rain still hammered the trailer. The wind gusted, rocking the trailer gently. At least it hadn't been tipped over, she thought gratefully.

Quietly she crept back to bed.

A phone ring woke her a couple of hours later. She looked around, wondering where it was. Spotting a phone on the dresser, she rose to answer it.

"Hello?" she said, still feeling half-asleep.

There was silence on the other end.

"Is anyone there?" she asked.

"Dani?" Connor's tone was incredulous.

"Yes." She stretched out the cord and made it back to bed, pulling the covers over her legs. It was too cold to stand.

"Where's Mick?"

"He's still asleep. Do you want me to wake him or can he call you back?"

"Busy night?"

"I'll say! How did you know?"

"Put Mick on."

His voice had become icy.

Dani frowned. "Okay." She kicked off the covers and pulled on her jeans. Fastening them as she headed for the living room, she wondered what was so urgent that Connor wanted to wake Mick. It was Saturday. Didn't the man ever take a day off?

"Mick?" She shook him gently. "Mick, Connor wants to talk to you." She shook him harder. He groaned and rolled onto his back, gazing up at her through half-closed eyes. "Tell him I'm still asleep."

"I tried."

She watched as he rose and went to the extension in the kitchen. He'd slept in his clothes, and she knew the sofa couldn't have been that comfortable.

She tiptoed back to the bedroom to hang up that receiver.

She quickly finished dressing, glad for the warmth of socks and shoes. She skirted by Mick and looked at his kitchenette. It was larger than hers and well equipped. She found coffee and began to prepare it. There was no tea. One cup wouldn't hurt, she rationalized, trying not to listen to Mick's side of the conversation.

Not that mumbled, half-asleep yeahs and nos weren't very revealing.

She saw Mick sit straight up. "What are you talking about?" he almost yelled.

Fascinated, Dani forgot about being discreet. Had something happened at the site in Pueblo?

Mick quickly recounted the events of last night, how she'd come to stay in his trailer, and included a report of damages she hadn't been aware of.

He waited a moment, then his tone softened.

"That's all right. When are you coming back? We could use some help here…. I don't know, one of the men was going to try to get to Carson Creek today. We need more chain saws than we have. It's a mess."

He looked at Dani. "I'll offer. What happens when you get here…? Okay. See you then." Mick hung up the phone and looked at her with a smile.

"Is that coffee I smell?" he asked.

"It should be ready in another minute or two. Is something wrong in Pueblo?" she asked.

"No. The storm barely reached them. And the wind doesn't seem as bad."

She couldn't very well ask what had gotten Connor so agitated. If Mick wanted her to know, he'd tell her.

When she handed him a cup of coffee later, she sat gingerly on the edge of a chair.

"Are you going to be able to get rid of that tree in my trailer today?"

"I don't know. We're going to try."

"I don't want to put you out again tonight. I can sleep in my living room if I have to."

Mick looked at her curiously. "Actually, Connor suggested you bunk in with him."

# Chapter Eighteen

"What?"

Surely Dani hadn't heard him correctly.

"He has an extra room. Might make some sense—just until we fix your trailer. Think about it at least."

She opened her mouth to refute the idea, then closed it. What could she say that wouldn't raise suspicions?

Could she move into Connor's trailer even temporarily? No matter how short-term, it was definitely a bad idea. She couldn't control her fantasies when eating dinner with the man. However would she cope, actually living under the same roof with him? They would share meals and living quarters. And every night she'd know he was only the thickness of a wall away.

She'd go crazy!

Sipping her coffee, she looked out the window at her trailer, studying the massive pine lying at a steep angle across the roof. Branches covered it like a thick, lacy tablecloth. The top of the tree hovered over Mick's trailer, but hers kept it from falling onto his. By craning her neck, she could see farther along the line of trailers toward the lake.

Branches littered the ground. Rain pelted puddles six feet wide. The trees continued to bend and sway in the strong wind. Watching them, she was amazed more hadn't fallen. They seemed to bend more than she would have thought possible. At what point would they snap and break like the one on her trailer?

Mick joined her a few minutes later. The older man had shaved and dressed, but still looked tired.

"How bad is it out there?" she asked.

"No one's hurt, but there's a lot of debris. Branches, mostly. A couple of trees. Once we get the one on your trailer cut away, we can assess the damage. Same with Joe Porter's trailer. It sustained heavy damage."

"If you can seal off the bedroom so the place will hold the heat, I can make do sleeping in the living room. The sofa's comfortable and it's only for another month. I don't need to stay in Connor's trailer. What happens when he returns?" Dani said, wondering if they would keep her on if she had no place to live.

She didn't relish making the thirty-mile trip from Carson Creek each day—especially if the weather was anything like today.

"We'll have to see how bad the damage is. If the propane lines were cracked or the electricity compromised, the place might be uninhabitable. Connor has the room."

"While he's gone, you mean?"

Mick cleared his throat. "Not only that. He has a bigger trailer than the rest of us—two bedrooms."

Dani grew suspicious. "Is he coming back?"

Mick nodded.

"And I'm to stay there with him?"

Dani didn't know whether to yell with frustration or quietly accept what looked like the way it was going to be.

"Plan to stay there at least until we know what to do with your place."

"And this won't give rise to problems with the men?"

"What are you talking about?"

"Connor didn't want me working here at all, if you'll remember, because my presence would prove disruptive. This wouldn't prove disruptive?"

Mick's eyes twinkled. "Only to Connor, I suspect. And it serves him right. It's good to see the man take an interest in something beyond the job at hand. Plan to stay a day or two. We'll be better able to assess the repairs needed once we get the tree removed."

It would serve the man right if she disrupted every aspect of his life, because he sure had disrupted hers.

For a moment, the thought made her smile.

She'd be the perfect guest. He'd never know she was there.

And if he wanted more kisses—well, he could find them elsewhere.

She would not give in.

And as soon as her trailer was ready, she'd move back so fast his head would spin.

At least that was her intention, until she actually packed up the few things she needed and headed for his trailer. Most were damp and she went to hang them to dry in Connor's bathroom, then stopped dead.

The man had a tub!

Visions of a warm bath had her smiling in delight. Staying with Connor would bring definite perks especially when he wasn't even home.

After dinner, Dani filled the tub with hot water. She'd carefully refrained from spending the entire day soaking in the tub. There were limits! Instead, she'd spent the day at the office, keeping track of reports of damage and repairs and reporting to Mick each time he came in. But lingering in the back of her mind was the lovely thought of the hot bath she'd have this evening.

By the time she'd prepared dinner, Connor still hadn't returned. Maybe he was waiting for the next morning, when it would be easier to navigate the muddy access road.

She'd made up the bed in the guest room and hung up her dried clothes. Carefully closing the bathroom door and locking it just in case Connor arrived home while she was using the tub, she slipped into the steaming water.

Bliss!

She soaked until the water turned cool, added more hot and stayed a bit longer. By the time she climbed from the tub, Dani was relaxed and warm through and through. She put on her long flannel nightgown and matching robe, dried her hair, then tidied up the bathroom. Except for the steamy air carrying the scent of her bubble bath, the place was as she'd found it.

She opened the door and knew immediately that Connor had returned. She hadn't heard him, but she felt his presence.

Tightening the belt on her robe, she hoped it covered everything. But with the mound of baby in front, she couldn't check below her waist.

"Dani?"

So much for the burgeoning hope that she could dash to her room and pretend to be asleep. Facing him in the morning when fully dressed sounded wiser than tonight in her gown and robe!

"You're home," she said brightly. Clutching her clothes in her arms, she walked down the short hall to the living room.

He seemed to fill the space in this large trailer as much as he did in her own, smaller place. Her heart gave a skip.

She'd missed him!

Gone a week and she'd missed him every moment.

The realization struck with the impact of a cement piling.

What would she do when the job was over and she never saw him again? Would she miss him the rest of her life?

The mere thought scared her. He could not become that important to her!

But she feared he had.

He looked tired. She wanted to wrap her arms around him, sooth away the stress and provide comfort.

Blinking, she tried to black out the image.

"How are things in Pueblo?" she asked, determined not to give in to the embarrassment that hovered. It was a good thing he couldn't read minds.

"Everything's progressing on schedule. How are you?"

"Fine." She smiled again, hoping this inane conversation would be the extent of their interaction tonight.

He crossed the room until he was almost touching her, crowding her, seeming to take the oxygen from the air. Raising his hand, he wound a curl around his finger, tugging gently.

"I saw your trailer. Thank God you weren't in bed when the tree came through."

She nodded, unable to say a word. Her senses were on overload, all from a gentle caress of a finger in her hair! She was aware of every nuance of his expression, the shadows in his eyes.

Clearing her throat, she tried to speak. "Can it be fixed?"

"I don't know. They were still working on getting the tree cut away when I arrived. They've stopped until morning. Is the guest room okay?"

She nodded, pulling against his finger. Dani placed her palm against his chest and pushed slightly. Slowly he unwrapped the curl. She could feel the heat of his body through the shirt, the pounding of his heart. She snatched her hand back.

"Mick said I should stay here. And I'll do it because I don't have much choice, but only until my trailer is fixed. I wouldn't want to be disruptive," she said firmly.

She needed to get that cleared up so there'd be no misunderstanding on either side.

He hesitated, then nodded once and stepped back. "Of course. Do you have everything you need?"

"Yes. I'm heading for bed now."

"Good night."

He turned and walked into the kitchen. Dani waited for something more, but she heard only the sound of the rain on the roof and then water running in the kitchen sink.

Disappointed that he hadn't challenged her comment, hadn't told her she could disrupt his life as much as she wanted, she headed for the guest room. She closed the door behind her and dumped her clothes on a chair and took off her robe.

What had she expected—that he would be so overcome with desire he'd brush aside her words and sweep her into a passionate embrace?

Ruefully, as she slipped between the covers, she admitted to herself that was exactly what she wished would happen.

What had he expected. Connor wondered, as the water poured down the sink. That she'd leap into his arms and beg him to kiss her again?

He gave a harsh laugh. She'd never done anything to indicate she wanted anything more than a boss-secretary relationship.

He was the one who had kissed her.

*But she responded,* came the whispered reply.

He shut off the tap, the coffeepot long since filled. Slowly he went through the motions of making coffee.

Dani was in the room down the hall, by now in bed. What did she wear to bed, something frilly and sexy? Or flannel, long and virginal? With her robe so tightly wrapped, he hadn't a clue.

Most people might not associate virginal with a woman who was seven months pregnant, but she had an aura about her that spoke of innocence and shyness.

He started the coffee maker, feeling anger at the man who had gotten her pregnant and then abandoned her. How could anyone do that to someone as sweet as Dani?

Sweet? Not when she was on a roll about something. Not when she stood up for herself or something she believed in.

But there was an overall sweetness about her that drew him like a moth to flame.

And was likely to produce the same result. If he weren't careful, the barriers would crumble and he'd be as exposed as he'd been when Catherine and Sammy were taken.

He rested his forearm on the cabinet and leaned his head against it. He was tired. Came from not getting a good night's rest in a week.

He'd thought—hoped—the distance from Dani would help him forget. Help him not yearn to kiss her, feel the silky texture of that beautiful blond hair. He'd hoped distance would allow him to gain some perspective.

Instead, he'd tossed and turned every night, wondering what she'd done during the day and what she was doing at that moment.

He didn't want to even think about his reaction that morning when she'd answered Mick's phone, sounding so sleepy. He'd known instantly he'd wakened her. But the searing pain that hit at the thought of her in bed with Mick had been totally unexpected. And not easy to erase.

Granted, Mick was old enough to be her father, but sometimes women went for older men.

It wasn't as if Connor had anything to offer her. Why should he care if Dani found someone else?

"Someone else?" he muttered, straightening and taking a cup from the cupboard. The coffee was almost ready. "As if she and I had something going on and she was turning away."

He'd had his shot at happiness. Stolen away by a gunman's bullet.

Dani deserved her own chance at happy ever after.

Connor took his cup and wandered to the large living-room window, staring out into the stormy night, all his senses attuned to the bedroom next to his. Was she already asleep? Should he knock on the door and tell her he didn't want to be roommates, that he wanted something more for the few weeks they'd remain on the job site?

And then what? Thanks for the memories? Have a good life?

He sighed and sipped the hot beverage. Life sucked sometimes.


Dani awoke early Sunday morning. It took a couple of moments to realize where she was. Rising, she wondered if Connor was still asleep. She opened her door slowly. The door to his room was shut. She quietly used the bathroom, then dressed. Venturing out into the main part of the trailer, she found it empty.

There was coffee in the pot, still hot. He must have gotten up before her. Was he already out? Or had he gone back to bed?

Dani had brought her tea and quickly made herself a cup. She debated fixing breakfast for them both, but decided that, without knowing what he liked, or even when he'd want it, doing so would waste food.

By ten o'clock she was bored. The high winds had abated and the torrential downpour eased. Rain was merely drizzling down now. Gray skies looked depressing. Connor had to have gone out. There was no sound from his bedroom.

Finally she decided she needed some company. Donning her jacket, she headed for the office.

Several men were gathered around the makeshift conference table, looking up in surprise when she entered. Connor was at his desk. Mick leaned against the wall, talking with the group.

"Anything wrong?" Connor asked.

"No. I wanted to see if I could do something to help."

"The rain's slowing. We should have the tree removed by the end of today," Mick said. "Pull up a chair. We're rehashing where we're behind and trying to come up with a plan to get us back on track."

She hung up her coat and moved to the seat one of the men vacated for her. Smiling in thanks, she sat, her gaze going immediately to Connor.

It felt right.

The thought scared her, but she couldn't help it. Being with him was what she wanted, even if she just sat on the sidelines and watched. And when he talked she had the perfect excuse to gaze her fill. Everyone else was looking at him, as well. No one would think anything of her own hungry gaze.

By the time the meeting broke up, Dani had her emotions firmly under control. She had her own assignments that she could start in the morning.

In the meantime, there was the afternoon to get through—and the evening.

When the other men filed out, she looked at Connor. "I'm going back to fix some lunch. Shall I fix it for you, too?"

His gaze caught hers, held. "That'd be nice, thanks."

She nodded, almost giddy with the thoughts that spun in her mind. She wanted to push Mick from the office, lock the door and get Connor to kiss her again.

Instead, Dani donned her coat and hurried from the office. The damp air felt good on her heated cheeks.

# Chapter Nineteen

By the time Connor stepped into the trailer a little later, Dani had lunch ready. Thick ham-and-cheese sandwich wedges filled the plates, with apples and carrots cut in bite-size pieces. There were brownies for dessert.

"You don't have to fix all the meals," he said as he sat at the small table with her.

"Lunch certainly isn't a problem. Consider it compensation for staying here."

He took a bite of a sandwich and chewed thoughtfully. "Your compensation for the job includes housing. Until your own place is fixed, this is housing. No need to pay for it."

"Okay. But I don't mind."

When they finished eating, Connor carried the plates into the kitchen and ran water on them.

"I can do the dishes," Dani said, following him in, carrying their beverage glasses. She placed them in the sink, bumping into him gently.

He seemed to freeze, then turned slowly. The water ran from the faucet. He ignored it as he put his wet hands on her shoulders and leaned over until his mouth covered hers.

Dani sank into the kiss as if she'd been waiting for it all her life. His mouth was warm and sexy, bringing her alive as she'd never been before. His lips were firm and demanding. She hungered for the excitement being with him brought. Longed for the kiss to go on forever.

"Ah, Dani," he said softly, gathering her closer, wrapping his arms around her, holding her snugly against him. Despite the baby between them, she felt as if she belonged just where she was.

She kissed him back, wishing she could burrow right under his skin and become a part of him. It was glorious kissing Connor. She reveled in the sweet, hot tingles of delight that coursed through her.

"Ah, Catherine," he said as he trailed kisses along her jaw line.

It was like a splash of icy water. Dani's eyes opened and drew back.

"*Catherine?*" she said.

"What?" Connor looked at her. "What are you talking about?"

"You just said 'Catherine.' I'm not Catherine, I'm Dani. You can't even keep your women straight!" She felt sick to her stomach. He was only using her as a substitute for his wife!

"No I didn't," he said.

She moved back against the counter and glared at him.

The sharp crack of a glass falling on the floor caused Dani to jump in surprise. It reminded her for a second of the tree falling. She felt as if she were falling—falling in love with the most unsuitable man in the world. A man who had no inclination for romance or commitment. And who was still in love with his dead wife.

He pulled back and looked at the shattered glass on the floor.

"Don't step on it," he warned, moving across the small area to reach for the broom.

She looked at the glass and slowly moved off the linoleum onto the carpet. There were a few shards there as well.

"That's impossible," Connor said as he swept up the broken pieces and then used the dustpan to collect them to dump in the trash.

Once done he advanced toward her.

"Stay away from me. I was nothing but a substitute for your wife. I can't believe I didn't realize it!" Dani spun around and ran for the sanctuary of her bedroom, slamming the door and turning the lock with a sharp snick. Leaning against it, she let the tears fall. The searing pain in her chest threatened to rip her in two.

Here she thought she was falling in love and the man in question yearned for another woman.

What a *fool* she'd been! How could she have imagined anyone would be so taken with a fat pregnant woman they'd want to woo her? How could she have been so gullible yet again?

Hadn't she learned anything from life?

"Dani." Connor knocked on the door, rattled the knob.

"Go away," she said, hoping he couldn't hear the tears in her voice.

"No. I want to talk to you."

"I don't want to talk to you. I'm packing. I'll be gone as soon as I can."

"No you won't. Where would you go? Open the door."

She pushed away and tried to see through her tears. She needed to leave. Not only the trailer, but the construction site, Carson Creek—maybe even Colorado. She couldn't stay, not after this.

Panic struck. What would she do without this job? It was highly unlikely anyone would offer her a job this close to her delivery date. She'd have no medical coverage, no income—and she still needed every penny she could scrape together. She couldn't lose her job over pride.

The door swung open.

She whirled around. "Get out!" How had he managed to unlock it?

"Not until we talk."

"There's nothing to talk about. I'm not Catherine!"

She almost screamed the words, the ache in her heart growing. Tears spilled down her cheeks. She hurt all over, and rubbing her aching chest, she tried to glare at him through the shimmering tears.

He stepped inside cautiously, moving closer until he was close enough to reach out and touch her if he wanted.

"I know you're not Catherine. There was only you and me in that kiss. Only you and me. If I said her name, I'm sorry. I wasn't thinking of her. I knew every second it was you in my arms."

Dani dashed the tears away and tried to hang on to the rage that filled her, if only to hold off the panic.

"Get out."

"Dani, don't cry. You're not a substitute for Catherine. Nor for anyone else. You are uniquely you. Special in your own right. I've wanted you for weeks. Why do you think I went to Pueblo?"

"To check on your precious project." She refused to be swayed by seductive words.

"To try to escape my growing interest in a blond secretary who was consuming too much of my mind," he replied.

"Well, you won't have that problem again. I'll get out of your life and you can go back to the way you were."

"I'll never be able to do that again," he said, reaching out to brush the tears from her cheek. "Don't cry, Dani. The last thing I wanted to do was make you cry."

"Get out," she whispered, holding on to a shred of control, longing to buy into his words and fling herself back into his arms. To feel that incredible sense of right and happiness that she'd had for so short a time minutes before.

But she'd been burned too often to risk it.

She just hoped she could get over it before the end of time.

"I'll leave, but not until I know you are all right," he said raggedly.

"I'm fine." She brushed away more tears, holding on to her control for all she was worth. She just wanted him out before she died of utter humiliation!

Connor turned and left, closing the door softly behind him.

She flung herself onto the bed, crying as if her heart was broken, which it very well might be.

Connor headed back to the living room. He went over every moment of their kiss unable to believe he'd said Catherine's name.

Had he really said Catherine's name?

If so, it was unforgivable.

Especially with someone like Dani, who didn't have a lot of good memories in her background. Who didn't have the self-confidence a woman would need to weather something like this.

He'd made no promises. She knew he wasn't planning on a long-term relationship, but anyone would be hurt to be a substitute for someone else.

Dani was nothing like Catherine.

Maybe he should tell her that. Prove he didn't mix them up.

He thought of the picture in the dresser drawer. Catherine's smile always delighted him. It still warmed his heart when he looked at her and Sammy.

But they were gone. They'd died, but he hadn't. Life went on.

And sometimes windows opened when doors closed.

Gazing off into space he knew he'd never forget them. They were an important part of his life and always would be.

But there was someone else now whom he'd hurt, and he needed to make amends any way he could.

Dani awoke when nature called. The baby seemed to be practicing for gymnastic events at the Olympics, she thought, as she opened the door a crack. Trying to keep her mind empty of images and regrets, she listened intently, hearing nothing. She crossed to the bathroom and quickly shut the door.

She peered into the mirror, dismayed at her swollen eyes, the blotchy color of her skin.

Darn, how was she going to ask Mick about her trailer repairs looking like this? If anyone saw her, speculation would run rampant and cause the very gossip and disruption Connor had warned against at the onset.

"Serves him right," she muttered.

But she wouldn't deliberately cause havoc on the site. He and Mick had been good enough to let her stay, to earn more money in these few weeks than she'd ever have earned in Denver.

If she'd let her expectations soar, it was her own fault when reality slapped her down.

She knew she was not meant for a permanent relationship— marriage and a big family. Today provided another example to hammer the fact home.

When she walked into the living room, she was startled to see Connor sitting on one of the chairs, staring out the window.

He turned when he heard her.

"Will my trailer be repaired soon?" she asked.

Her heart pounded, and her mind tumbled with memories—of how he had kissed her, touched her so gently. The delight they'd shared. She closed down tightly. She dared not go there!

"We need to have an insurance adjuster look at it. But it's unlikely we'll repair it this year. The damage is more severe than we first thought."

She took a deep breath. "I need the trailer."

"We've listened to the long-range weather forecasts and it looks as if we only have another week or two of passable weather to work. There's another storm coming in next week, and another expected immediately after that. They're arctic, so they'll be bringing snow. We'll be working flat out to get as much completed and enclosed before we have to suspend operations. There's no time to fix the trailer."

"I can't stay here," she almost whispered.

"You're safe here, Dani. I won't touch you again."

She swallowed and looked out the window.

"If it makes you feel better, I'll bunk in with Mick," he offered unexpectedly.

She looked at him again. "That would give rise to speculation, wouldn't it?"

He shrugged. "Either way, the men will talk."

"Maybe I should leave altogether."

"We'll only be here another couple of weeks, max. Stay and I'll throw in bonus money."

She hesitated.

A hard light entered his eyes. "Stay until the end. You've straightened out the office and everything's up to date and running smoothly. I'd like to close the year out that way."

Nodding, she turned to walk to the kitchen. Maybe a cup of tea would help. At least it gave her something to do. Awkward hardly described how she felt. Embarrassed and mortified came close.

And sad.

And the worst of it was, she still was so very aware of the man.

He followed her into the kitchen.

"Want to talk?" Connor asked.

Dani shook her head. There was nothing to talk about.

"I'm going out then." He hesitated a moment. "Plan to stay until we close up for the winter. I won't bother you again. We'll be roommates, nothing more."

She nodded, her gaze fixed firmly on the teakettle, as if watching it intently would hasten its boiling.

He waited another moment, then left.

Dani listened to him cross to the front door, open it and go out. With the sound of it closing, she knew she was alone.

In one sense she'd always been alone—from the moment her mother had delivered her to social services. Yet Dani kept hoping this time would be a magic time.

When was she going to learn?

It was easy enough to avoid Connor the rest of the day. She took snacks and drinks to her room, climbed into bed and read. Fortifying herself proved unnecessary, for he hadn't returned by the time she went to sleep.

Monday the rain had stopped, though the sky was gray and dreary. Water dripped from the trees as if it were still raining.

Dani dressed warmly and headed for the office. Either Connor had not spent the night in the trailer or he'd come in late and left early. She saw no evidence of his presence while she prepared her breakfast.

Mick was the only person in the office when she entered. She ignored the twinge of disappointment and went straight to her desk after a murmured good-morning. She was glad she didn't have to face Connor.

"Sorry about your trailer, Dani. Connor said he told you we can't fix it," Mick said, reaching for his hard hat. "Can you get the rest of your things from it today? We want to have it hauled out of here and down to a repair shop before the weather gets any worse. The insurance adjuster will be coming out tomorrow to examine it. After that, we'll leave it in Carson Creek until spring."

"Sure."

He hesitated at the door. "I'm needed outside. Are you all right?"

She nodded and smiled, trying to convey the image of a woman who had everything going just the way she wanted in life.

"Did Connor tell you we're down to the wire now? Only another two weeks left and we'll close for the winter."

She nodded again, her smile feeling tight and phony. Couldn't he tell?

"You all right with that? We thought we might get more time in."

"It'll give me plenty of time to find an apartment and settle somewhere before the baby comes. Anything special you want me to do today?"

"Just keep on doing what you've been doing."

When Mick left, Dani sat back in her chair. Two weeks. In two weeks they'd all go their separate ways. Would she ever see Connor after that?

# Chapter Twenty

She expected him to stay away from her after yesterday afternoon, so Dani was surprised that evening when he entered the trailer shortly after she had begun to prepare dinner. She'd set a stew to simmering during her long lunch break, running across several times in the afternoon to check on it.

She'd just put cornbread into the oven when he arrived.

"Something smells good," he said easily.

The wary look in his eyes belied his casual tone.

"I fixed a stew and have cornbread baking. It'll be ready soon if you want some."

There was plenty if he chose to join her. If he refused, she could reheat leftovers later in the week.

"Do I have time enough for a shower?"

She nodded, taking a slow breath. Maybe they could coexist for the next couple of weeks.

Dani was surprised at the degree of contentment his arrival induced. She still felt raw from yesterday, but a part of her wanted to be with him, no matter what the cost. She only had a few more days.

Dinner consisted entirely of casual conversation that could have been held between total strangers. Connor never came near enough to even accidentally brush against her. Never said a word that the entire world couldn't have heard.

And as soon as they were finished, he headed back out, claiming he had work to do at the office.

That set the pattern for the week. He was gone every morning before she awoke, and after a hasty dinner, disappeared each evening.

Dani did her best to keep to her room when he was in the trailer, but felt more lonely than before.

On Friday, she had another appointment with her new doctor. She left for Carson Creek right after lunch, driving carefully on the gravel road into town. Evidence of the storm was everywhere. In one spot a tree had fallen across the road. The construction crew had the center cut out to allow traffic to pass, both ends still lying on the roadsides. There were puddles in the ruts, and more mud than she remembered.

Still, the trip proved uneventful. Once her appointment was concluded, she headed for the only general merchandise store in town.

She hadn't bought anything for her baby and wanted to get an idea of what was available and how much it all cost.

Wandering through the small department, Dani was enchanted with the tiny garments, the fancy dresses for little girls and the miniature jeans for boys. What would her baby be? Girl or boy?

The prices concerned her a bit. A crib wasn't cheap, yet it was necessary. Some of the little jump suits and sleepers were inexpensive, but she knew babies grew fast.

It was the teddy bear that captured her fancy, so soft, floppy and cuddly that she couldn't resist. It seemed extravagant to purchase a toy when the baby needed more practical things. But she bought it, anyway. Life was not all about practicality.

When she left the shop, she debated about driving back or stopping to eat dinner first. Eating would mean she'd be driving home in the dark on that barely passable road.

Yet she craved a pizza. She hadn't had any in weeks and loved it. Pregnant women had cravings. Hers hadn't been outrageous, but she wanted pizza tonight! She'd indulge her craving as soon as she put her packages in the trunk.

She almost jumped when she saw Connor leaning against the side of her car, his arms folded across his chest, his gaze fixed firmly on her as she walked toward him.

She slowed her pace, uncertain what he was doing here.

"Hi," she said when she reached him.

"What do you think you're doing, driving here by yourself?"

Irritation rose. "I'm perfectly capable of driving myself to Carson Creek. It's none of your business."

"I could have brought you in. I'll follow you home."

"I don't need a keeper, Connor," she said, oddly touched that, despite everything, he'd come after her to make sure she was safe.

"Apparently you do." He stepped aside to let her into the car.

"I'm not going home yet. I'm going to have dinner here in town."

"I'll wait."

She stared at him, and his implacable expression let her know that's exactly what he would do. He could be so stubborn.

But so could she.

"Actually, I'm going for pizza," she said finally. "Do you want pizza for dinner?" It wasn't quite an invitation, but it was the best she could do.

She still heard Catherine's name on his lips echoing in her

mind.

He hesitated a moment. Dani's heart dropped. No, he didn't want to have dinner with her.

"Pizza sounds good."

He glanced up the street and spotted the local pizza parlor. "That place?"

"The only one in town, I think."

They walked up the sidewalk. The shopping bag hung from her fingers. She should have stowed it.

It was too early for the Friday night crowd so the restaurant was practically empty. There were booths along one wall, picnic-style tables down the middle with bench seats. Only a few families and couples were present.

"Booth?" Connor asked.

Dani nodded and led the way to the first empty one. She slid in one side and he slid into the other. They studied the posted menu on the far wall and decided on a combination pizza. Connor went to place their order and returned with a pitcher of cola and two glasses.

"I assumed no beer," he said as he sat back down.

"Not for me."

"Me, neither."

He poured their drinks. Silence descended.

Connor studied her as she looked around. Looked every where but at him, actually.

He noticed the bag beside her.

"What did you buy?" he asked.

She glanced at him almost shyly, a small smile lighting her features. Pulling out the brown floppy bear, she sat it on the table. "A teddy bear for the baby. Isn't it darling?"

She gazed at the toy as if it was the most precious thing in creation.

Connor could envision her looking at her baby the same way.

He felt as if he'd been kicked in the gut with a steel-toed work boot. Dani was the sweetest woman he'd ever met. He'd kissed her, tasted her sweetness, felt every inch of that incredibly soft, womanly body pressed against his

Startled, he realized he wanted her to look at him with that same gaze she gave a teddy bear.

How could he have hurt her so badly? What could he do to make up for it? He almost ached to reach across and touch her. To have her smile at him.

Her vulnerability hit him square in the chest. She was alone in the world, with no family, no close friends he'd seen evidence of. Yet she was looking forward to her baby and to making a home.

"It's foolish, I know, to buy a teddy bear before the baby's even born. And who knows how long it'll be before he or she can play with it? But I couldn't resist."

"How about other things?"

"I looked at them." Some of the delight went out of her face. "Everything's more expensive than I expected."

"Probably here in Carson Creek—they have to pay more to have it shipped in. You should shop in other places, find a discount house with better bargains. Or order on-line."

She nodded, replacing the bear in the bag.

Connor hesitated a long moment, then slowly said, "Sammy's crib is still at my folks'. You could have that if you want."

He stared at her stunned expression, feeling stunned himself. How could he offer his son's crib to a stranger?

Not a stranger. Dani.

"Are you sure?"

He nodded. "We could go this weekend and pick it up."

Where had that come from? He hadn't been back to Fort Collins since he'd sold his house and left for that first remote job site, three years ago. He'd never intended to return.

She stared at him warily. "Fort Collins is clear across the state, almost in Wyoming."

"I know where it is," he replied calmly.

His manner belied the sudden tension ratcheting up inside him. Was he crazy? He hadn't been home in years. Was he up to facing Fort Collins and all its memories?

"It'd take all day to get there and all day back," she said.

He should take that as an out. But he didn't.

"That's right. We'll head out tomorrow, stay Sunday and return on Monday."

Dani started to say something just as his name rang out from the serving counter.

Connor rose and went to get their pizza. He snagged two plates and a few packets of hot sauce.

Had he lost his mind? The last thing he wanted to do was return to Fort Collins.

Yet he couldn't stand seeing Dani distressed. And it had nothing to do with his own part in insulting her by saying Catherine's name. He wanted to help her. Wanted to make things easier if he could.

She could use a few breaks in life.

When he placed the pizza on the table, she looked up at him, wariness still evident in her gaze.

"Then I say thank-you. I appreciate it. But maybe we ought to wait until I decide on a place to live first. No sense bringing the crib here if I decide to settle back in Denver."

"I don't know how long the roads will be clear. Better to go tomorrow."

She hesitated only a moment, then nodded. "Okay."

They ate the pizza with gusto. Dani darted puzzled glances at him from time to time, as if she wasn't sure she'd heard him correctly.

No wonder, he thought. Normally he didn't do things so spontaneously. Maybe that's what his life needed these days—more spontaneity.

"We'll have to take my truck," he said, "so we can carry the crib back."

She nodded.

"I'll call my folks. We'll stay with them."

She widened her eyes at that. "Should I? I could get a motel room somewhere."

"Why would you do that?"

"Won't they think it odd, you showing up with me?"

He looked at the piece of pizza he was about to eat and shrugged. "They probably will be so glad to see me they won't care who's with me." He glanced up. "I didn't mean that quite as it came out. You'll be welcomed."

Maybe this would ease the hurt he'd inflicted.

Of course, the penance might be more than he could bear.

For the first time he thought of what returning to Fort Collins would mean. He hadn't been back since that awful time. Would things have changed? Or look the same, be the same except for the loss of Catherine and Sammy?

Connor led the way back to the construction site. Dani was glad for the bright headlights filling the road ahead. She stayed close, grateful the man had come, after all.

When they parked their vehicles, Mick came from his trailer. "Where have you two been?" he called, walking over.

"Had dinner in town," Connor said. He opened the door to his trailer and motioned them both in. Dani passed so close she could feel the heat from his body.

Feeling slightly shaken, she lifted the bag. "I'll put this away."

Escaping to her room, she was glad for the brief respite.

Shedding her jacket, she hung it up and took the teddy bear from the bag, setting it on her bed. Smiling, she recaptured some of the happiness she'd had shopping. When she turned to rejoin the men, Mick's voice stopped her in her doorway.

"What do you mean, you're going to Fort Collins? You haven't been there since Catherine died."

"Dani needs a crib, and Sammy's is at my folks' place. I'm giving it to her."

"Connor, we have two weeks before we close down. There's too much to do. You can't just take off for three days."

"You can handle it."

"Why now? Why not later?"

"You said it yourself. In two weeks we close down. I'm heading for Boulder and that project until it's completed. Dani will be off somewhere else. When would I get it for her?"

"Anytime after the next two weeks. I'll go up and get it then."

"I don't expect to see her again after we close up for winter," Connor said firmly. "We're going tomorrow."

Dani crossed her arms over her chest, hugging herself in disappointment. Stupid, she chided herself. Had she thought that, just because he'd offered her the crib, anything had changed?

No wonder he wanted to go so soon. He wanted nothing to extend their time together. In two weeks they'd say goodbye, and that would be that.

She should refuse to go. Tell him she'd changed her mind, that she didn't need anything from him and would manage fine on her own. His first duty was to the job, not to his temporary secretary.

But cribs were expensive.

And this one would be a tie to Connor.

She turned and slowly closed the door, too dispirited to face the men, after all. Maybe things would look different in the morning. And she had until then to tell Connor she couldn't go.

# Chapter Twenty-One

It was still dark when Connor pounded on her door the next morning. Dani woke and sat up. Was there an emergency?

"Yes?"

He opened the door and stuck his head in, the light from the hall providing illumination.

"We didn't decide what time to leave, but I wanted an early start. Can you be ready to go soon?"

She opened her mouth to tell him she wasn't going, after all. He didn't wait for an answer, but pulled the door shut quickly.

Two seconds later Dani jumped from the bed and switched on the light. Okay, decision made. She'd go. She needed the crib and he wouldn't have offered if he didn't want her to have it.

And, she admitted, she wanted to spend time with Connor. They had only two more weeks. Wouldn't she be an idiot to give up a moment with him before she had to?

They were on the road within the hour, after eating a quick breakfast. Dani had dressed in record time and thrown a few things into a suitcase, which Connor put in the back of the truck cab. She still wasn't sure she should be going off for the entire weekend with the man.

"We'll stop somewhere along the way for a snack and lunch," he said as they climbed the hill from the construction site.

"We'll be stopping more than that," she murmured, glancing at him to judge his reaction.

He laughed.

Dani's heart skipped a beat. He was so gorgeous when he smiled. She'd seen him laugh only a couple of times. It always changed his features until she thought him the most beautiful thing she'd ever seen. She tried to imprint every detail of his face on her mind. She never wanted to forget Connor.

"I know about pregnant women and their bathroom needs," he said. "Just let me know when."

She nodded, not feeling embarrassed as she'd thought she might.

"I called my folks last night to let them know to expect us. They weren't home. I tried a neighbor and found out they're gone for the weekend," Connor said casually. "I thought they'd be home."

"Oh."

He flicked her a quick glance but didn't say anything more.

Dani gazed out the window, wondering why, after staying in his trailer with him for over a week, the thought of going to his family home unchaperoned made her feel so daring. It wasn't as if there was anything between them. Just her own awareness and yearnings. But he'd proved she didn't mean a thing to him.

Connor was still in love with his dead wife.

It was slow going along the curvy mountain roads, but once they reached the interstate, they made good time, despite Dani's request to stop every couple of hours. It was dinnertime and already growing dark by the time they headed into Fort Collins.

Dani was aware of the tension rising as Connor slowly drove into town. She looked at him, but his gaze was firmly fixed on the road in front of them.

She didn't say a word until he pulled into a driveway and cut the motor.

From what she could see in the waning daylight, the house was a nice ranch style in a lovely older neighborhood. Tall trees lined the streets, and the lawns were wide and nicely kept.

"This is it," he said.

"You grew up here?"

He nodded. "My folks bought this when Randy was just a baby." He looked at her. "He's my older brother, lives in Alaska." Slowly Connor raised his gaze and looked around, the tension seeping away.

"Let's unload, freshen up and go for dinner."

Dani nodded in agreement. It couldn't be easy for Connor to be here. Maybe he'd want to leave first thing in the morning. If his parents weren't home, there was no reason for him to stay in Fort Collins beyond picking up the crib.

The house was comfortably furnished. As he showed her to a bedroom, Dani glanced around, noticing the plush sofa that looked as if it called to be sat on. A large-screen TV sat against the wall, beside a stereo system that looked state of the art. Pictures on the walls gave the place a homey feeling.

The room he showed her to was obviously a guest room—impersonal, yet furnished with everything a visitor would need.

"The bath is across the hall. My room's next door. This was Randy's. Mom changed both of the rooms when we moved out."

"So no teenage memorabilia?" she teased.

"Packed in the garage. Wait until you see it. The place would put the Smithsonian to shame. She has her dolls from when she was a kid, and some old toys of Dad's that Grandma gave her.

Plus all my stuff and Randy's. Mom never throws anything away."

Dani smiled wistfully. She had nothing from when she'd been little, not even clear memories of her mother.

Did Connor have any idea how lucky he was?

"I'll be ready in a few minutes," she said, stepping inside the lovely room and firmly pushing away the wistful yearnings that rose.

"Take your time. I'll be in the living room when you're ready."

She put her overnight case on the small chair near the window and opened it. She hung up the shirts, put the jeans in the drawer and arranged her cosmetics on the dresser. She brushed her hair, going to stand by the window.

The backyard must have been a child's dream. Huge old trees provided limbs for a swing and tree house. Peering closely, she saw there was indeed a platform nestled in the sturdy branches. From when the boys were young, she knew.

A pang of regret struck her.

She wished she had more to offer her baby—a history of a loving family going back generations. Places they could visit that held meaning. People who had known her all her life.

Instead, it would be Dani and her baby against the world.

"Not to worry, little one," she said, rubbing her tummy gently. "We'll make our own traditions and make memories to last a lifetime."

When she walked into the living room, Connor was standing at the big window, staring out.

"Are you all right?" she asked.

He turned and nodded. "Just thinking."

"Mick said once you hadn't been home in three years. Do

you want to leave in the morning?"

He hesitated a moment, then slowly shook his head. "I want to show you around Fort Collins. You might like it here, might want to settle here instead of in Carson Creek. It's still got a small-town atmosphere, but has more to offer than Carson Creek, and it's a lot closer to Denver."

Settle in the one place Connor avoided? She didn't think so. Not that he'd come back to Carson Creek, but she could always hope. She smiled and shrugged her shoulders.

"Come on, let's go find something to eat," he suggested. "What would you like?"

"Anything, as long as there's a lot of it. I'm starved."

Dani was trying to recapture the feeling of friendship that had begun before their disastrous kiss. Connor seemed to be trying, as well. She wouldn't think about what might have been, but concentrate on what was.

He took her to a family restaurant a block off the main street. It served a wide assortment of entrées. She chose baked ham, while Connor chose rare steak.

"So tell me all about growing up in Fort Collins," she invited when their food arrived.

"It's a good place for kids, safe."

Then, as if he realized what he'd said, and how his own son had died, he stopped. "Most of the time, that is. It was when I was growing up."

"And it should have been for your son. I'm sorry," she said, feeling the helpless frustration of being able to do nothing to ease his pain.

"A random act of violence. Fort Collins is a great place, still safe for children."

"So if I settled here, where should I look? Your parents' neighborhood would be too expensive on a secretary's salary.

Always supposing I could get a job in a few months."

"I know some people in town. I can put in a good word," he said.

She nodded, once again feeling disappointment. Why did she keep hoping for more than came her way? What had she expected him to say—no need to worry, you'll have a job with us in the spring?

Yes, that was exactly what she'd wanted him to say!

"The Cutter Hill section is nice. Lots of apartment buildings there and the schools are good. We could drive over there tomorrow, if you like. So you could see the area."

"I would, thank you," she said.

Slowly Connor began to speak of things he and his brother had done as children. Of the freedom they'd enjoyed once they had bikes. Of Randy's getting a car when he was sixteen and how he'd let Connor ride around with him despite some of the protests of his cool friends. When Connor got his license, Randy had even let him borrow it—until he got his own wheels.

She laughed at the way Connor portrayed their constant battles to keep those old clunkers running, and the two times he'd gotten a ticket and had his father come down hard on him.

Connor spoke of fishing and skiing and family vacations.

Dani soaked it all in. To her, it sounded like the perfect life for a child. Just like the one she wanted her own baby to be able to look back on.

"Denver was different, I bet," he said perceptively at one point.

She nodded. "And not having one family to grow up with sure puts a different spin on things."

He reached out and took her hand.

Dani went still, startled by the tingling sensations racing through her. He didn't mean anything to her. She couldn't let

Connor mean anything.

But he did, and idiot that she was, she cherished every second spent with him, relished every touch. She met his gaze and almost caught her breath when she saw his expression.

She didn't know whether to wish she'd never met Connor or wish he would never let her go.

"Neither of us can change the past, but we have to go on. You'll be a wonderful mother to your baby, and give it a great life."

Her heart melted. "Thank you."

She let her hand stay in his, wishing he'd pull her into his arms, kiss her and hold her so tightly she could imagine he'd never let her go.

But he merely squeezed her hand slightly and released it.

By the time they returned home, Dani had her emotions firmly under control.

"Thanks for dinner," she said. "What time should I get up in the morning?"

"Are you ready for bed so soon? It's not even ten," Connor said, closing the front door behind him. He leaned on it, crossing his arms and regarding Dani.

"I'm tired from the drive. But I'll be ready to start early if you want."

He shook his head. "Sleep in as long as you like. The garage will be waiting whenever we get to it."

She bade him a quiet good-night and walked down the hall to the guest bedroom. Sleep proved elusive, however, with so many thoughts of Connor swirling in her mind.

Connor awoke early the next morning. It felt odd to be back in the room he'd had as a kid. His mom had changed everything except the placement of the window. He could still see the limbs of the old oak silhouetted against the dawn sky. He and Randy had used that old tree as a fort, for swings, for playing Tarzan.

He'd always thought Sammy would enjoy it as much.

Disliking the trend of his thoughts, he rose and showered. Listening by Dani's door for a moment assured him she was still asleep. He headed for the kitchen. It didn't take long to prepare coffee and he poured a cup of the hot brew as he gazed out the kitchen window into the backyard. But his thoughts were a long way away from the play area of his childhood.

Rousing himself, he finished the coffee and went for his jacket and car keys. He'd visit the bakery over on Elm Street and get something for breakfast.

The small strip mall that housed the bakery also held a dry-cleaning establishment and a florist. The clerk at the flower store was setting out buckets of fresh flowers when he drove into the parking lot.

He bought an assortment of croissants and sweet rolls, not knowing what Dani might like. On his way back to the car, he hesitated, eyeing the flowers.

Ten minutes later Connor turned slowly into the gravel driveway of the cemetery. It was deserted this early on a Sunday morning. Frost still dusted the grass, and the trees, denuded of their leaves, looked bleak. He stopped and climbed out, picking up the two bouquets.

Walking toward the monument he recognized, he was surprised to see that the earth wasn't raw and red, but grass had covered the places his loved ones lay.

Flowers just past their prime were in the containers by the headstones. Someone had been there recently.

Suddenly he felt guilty. He'd avoided coming for three years, while others had visited.

"Hi, Catherine," he said softly, pulling out the wilting flowers and putting the bouquet of red roses into the vase. There was still some water in it.

He had nothing else to say. She wasn't here. Her laughter danced on the wind. Her smile warmed his heart, but never again would he see it on her face. Her touch was but a memory.

The searing pain he expected was missing. Poignant memories flooded, but they were of happy times. They'd had a lot of happy times.

He moved to the tombstone next to hers. The little lamb on top would have pleased Sammy, Connor thought, placing the bouquet of daisies and carnations in the holder. A kid would like daisies, he thought, brushing the lamb gently. Maybe it should have been a puppy. Sammy had wanted a puppy so badly. Connor and Catherine had decided that when he was a little older they'd get a dog.

Connor wished they'd bought it that summer.

Swallowing hard, his eyes filling with tears, he gazed down at the ground. He missed them.

He loved them.

*Time to move on.*

He blinked and took a deep breath.

It was time to move on. Neither Catherine nor Sammy would have wanted him, or anyone, to grieve forever.

And he had moved on. He had a good job, a few friends. All he needed.

*What about love and laughter?*

The words seemed whispered on the wind.

He touched Catherine's tombstone and turned to walk away.

Coming here hadn't been as hard as he'd thought. He would never again fear to visit. The initial pain had faded, just as his mom had said it would. Now only the familiar ache remained.

When Connor entered the kitchen, Dani was sipping a cup of tea. She looked at him warily.

"I went to get breakfast," he said, holding up the white bag. "And to the cemetery."

"Oh, Connor." She rose and came to his side, reaching for his hand and squeezing it gently. "That must have been hard."

Her eyes were bright with sympathy, her voice soothing.

"Not as hard as I thought it would be."

He took a breath, threading his fingers through Dani's and holding on.

"They've been gone a long time and life moves on."

She nodded, her warmth just what he needed to dispel the cold.

"Hungry?" he asked.

"As ever." Slowly she pulled her hand away. "Is the coffee still good? Or shall I make some fresh?"

"It'll be fine. I bought an assortment of things because I didn't know what you'd like." He dumped the contents of the bag on a plate and pushed it into the middle of the table—croissants, muffins, rolls and cinnamon buns.

"This is nice," she said, choosing a croissant. "I'm sorry I didn't get to meet your parents."

He nodded in acknowledgment. "Did you ever try to find your parents once you were grown?" he asked.

He'd been thinking more and more about her childhood as he compared his own to hers.

She shook her head. "I thought about it. I fantasized about both parents finding me, that they'd been searching for me ever since I was little." She looked into his eyes. "I pretended they'd known they'd made a mistake and were trying to rectify it."

She shrugged and broke off a bit of pastry. "But it was a kid's fantasy. They knew what they were doing. If they didn't want me, I didn't want to know them. So I never looked."

"They missed a lot," he said softly.

She beamed at him. "Connor, that's the nicest thing anyone has ever said to me!"

He frowned, balled up his napkin and rose. "It's true. You ready to tackle the garage? I don't know where the crib will be. We might have to move half the contents to get to it. Wait until you see the stuff Mom keeps."

"I stand ready to help!" Dani said, jumping up and clearing their dishes.

"Leave those until later. And I don't need help. You shouldn't be lifting or pushing anything heavy."

"Yes sir!" She snapped a sassy salute.

Connor felt a stir of desire at the laughter on her face. She was so pretty. Did she know that? He didn't think she had a clue.

He ached at the thought of a lonely little girl always hoping her parents would come for her. Life was unfair too often.

Turning before he could get caught up in her laughter, he headed for the garage.

Dani put on her jacket and followed.

Connor raised the large door to allow more light and make space to move things around. He sighed when he looked at all the boxes and pieces of furniture his mother saved.

"Wow," Dani said from beside him, peering into the crammed garage.

"She could probably supply the needs of a small third-world country with what she has here," he muttered, stepping in.

He tugged and pushed boxes around, stacking some on the driveway. Dani read the labels and wondered at all the things Connor's mother had deemed worthy of saving.

"Here it is," he called. Two more trips carrying boxes, and then he brought out the frame of a crib. It was wrapped in a sheet, which Connor stripped away. The oak finish was in perfect condition, the spindles set close together to prevent a baby's head from getting caught. He leaned it against a stack of boxes and went back in. A moment later he returned with the mattress and springs. The mattress had been wrapped in plastic, but the springs were dusty.

A car drove down the street and pulled into the driveway, stopping at the stack of boxes. Connor looked up, then went on alert.

What was George Andrews doing here? Had he come to see Connor's parents? Or had he learned Connor was in town?

Dani stepped closer. "Company?"

"Catherine's father."

The older man climbed from the sedan and glanced around, his eyes fastening on Dani for a long moment. He looked at Connor, questions in his eyes.

"It's been a while, son," he said.

Connor nodded, but didn't move forward to greet his former father-in-law. The embezzlement by his son stood in their way.

George closed the distance and held out his hand.

Connor gripped it in greeting.

The older man looked at Dani. "Your mother didn't tell me you'd remarried."

Connor frowned. "I haven't. This is Dani Winthrop. She's...a friend."

Dani smiled politely.

The older man nodded, then turned back to Connor. "I need to talk to you, son."

Connor knew what was coming and didn't want to deal with it. "About Marshal?"

George nodded. "Maybe we could go inside and discuss the matter." He flicked a glance at Dani.

"Dani knows all about it. She's my secretary at the construction site."

Connor did not say she'd been the one to discover the discrepancies. It didn't change anything.

"Things have been tough since Catherine died. We need to discuss how to handle the situation. Family should stick together in hard times. Catherine would have wanted that," the older man said.

"Catherine would not have condoned theft," Connor said evenly.

George flinched, hesitated, then nodded. "You're right. But she would have wanted to help her brother."

"It's out of my hands."

"But you could say something to mitigate the charges. Heck, I'll pay back the money. You won't be out a dime."

"It isn't me calling the shots. J&J Construction and Windhaven are the ultimate victims. And neither is giving any ground."

"Family always came first with Catherine. She'd want you to help out here, Connor. She'd be disappointed in you."

Connor nodded slowly. "I think you're right. And I plan to change that. But not by helping Marshal."

"What are you talking about?"

"I can't do anything for Marshal. He embezzled the money,

got caught, has to pay the piper. But I can stop living my life as if it stopped the same time Catherine's and Sammy's did. That's where I think she would have been disappointed in me."

George shook his head. "I'd hoped for better from you."

"Sorry, I can't compromise on what's right," Connor said in a hard voice.

The older man frowned and turned abruptly heading for his car without another word.

When he was gone, Dani looked at Connor. He seemed so alone.

"Catherine would have been proud that you stood up for what's right," she said.

He looked at her. "You think?"

She nodded. "Definitely."

"You never met her."

"Doesn't matter. I know you, so I can imagine the kind of woman you'd marry."

"She always fought injustice. I think letting someone get away with a crime would be the height of injustice."

# Chapter Twenty-Two

Dani wished Catherine's father hadn't come. They'd been enjoying the morning, talking easily as Connor moved boxes. Now he seemed to withdraw.

"Let's get the crib in the truck," he said, reaching for the springs.

When it was loaded, he turned back to the garage, bypassing the boxes stacked on the driveway. A moment later, he came out with another large cardboard box. Placing it on top of two others, he ripped off the sealing tape.

Opening it, he gestured to Dani. She peered inside.

Neatly folded baby clothes.

"Oh, aren't they sweet?" She drew one sleeper from the stack. It was so small. She held it up and smiled. "Hard to imagine a baby would fit in this, isn't it?"

He nodded, staring at the sleeper.

She folded it and put it back, looking at Connor, then at the box of baby clothes. Sammy's, obviously. Why had he brought it out?

"They're from the first year, I think. If you can use them, you can have them."

"Oh, I couldn't."

"Why not?"

"Don't you want them?"

"I don't need baby clothes. And they don't hold any special memories. Unlike my mother, I don't save everything that ever passed through my life."

"But one day you might want them."

He studied her for a moment, then shook his head. "No, I won't."

Dani knew from Mick that Connor didn't plan to marry again, but still, what if something happened and he changed his mind?

"Thank you," she said.

She wouldn't look for obstacles. He'd offered and she could use them. Gently she rubbed her fingertips over the soft cotton.

"We can take the box inside and you can look at all the different outfits, decide if you don't want some."

"I'd love to see every one." But she knew she'd take them all. The quality was good. Babies outgrew clothes the first year long before they could be worn out.

When her baby outgrew the outfits, she could pass them on. Or save them, in case Connor ever wanted them back.

He carried the box inside and left Dani with it while he went to restack the other boxes in the garage. She drew out sleepers and gowns, receiving blankets and sheets for the crib. She separated the piles and fingered the dainty clothes with excitement.

Soon her own baby would be wearing these things. She or he would kick her or his legs in the sleepers, wear the corduroy crawlers, the striped T-shirts. There were few things specifically for a boy. Almost everything could be worn by a girl just as easily. Granted, there were no dresses, and if she had a little girl, Dani would want to dress her up once in a while. But this was such a boon. Connor had saved her a lot of money, plus indecision about what to get.

Now she needed only to find a place to live, get the nursery set up and prepare for her baby's arrival.

Dani napped after lunch. Once she awoke, Connor suggested they drive around Fort Collins.

"I'll start with the Cutter Hill section. I think you'd fit in there," he said as they climbed into the truck.

"Will the crib be okay in back?"

"It can't fall out and no one will take it."

They drove through the downtown area, then out to the different neighborhoods of Fort Collins. It was a pretty town. Dani knew it'd look even lovelier in the summer when all the trees were in full leaf and flowers bloomed in gardens. Maybe she should consider living here.

"Thank you for showing me around," she said at one point in the afternoon. "I know this can't be easy for you."

"Why not? It's my hometown."

"I know, but you haven't been back in three years."

He reflected a moment. "True. I thought it'd be too hard. But it's not. I have a lot of good memories."

Just then they turned the corner and he stopped at the side of the road, looking at a brick elementary school.

"That's where a crazed man killed five people."

He stared at it for a long time. "I never considered how hard it must have been for all those children who saw the killings to return to school. For the teachers to resume their teaching."

He was silent for a long moment.

"It's just a building, not an evil spot in the world. A tragic thing happened there, but it was over in seconds. And lightning never strikes in the same place twice. It's probably the safest school in the country," he said at last.

Dani touched his hand, moved when he gripped hers hard in return.

"Let's go find something to eat. I'm hungry," she said.

She wanted to leave the school. Wanted Connor to leave the terrible memories behind.

They ate at a Mexican restaurant that Connor said was a favorite. The music was loud and they almost had to shout to be heard—until he moved from across the table to the chair next to hers. Bending their heads close together, they could talk without the need to yell.

Dani felt the familiar flutter when he leaned near. She longed to reach out and touch him. Twice when she'd offered comfort, he'd latched on to her hand, not rebuffed her as she'd feared he might.

But she wanted more than that.

And knew better than to tempt fate.

Dinner turned out better than she'd anticipated. Connor seemed happier than anytime she'd seen him. It seemed as if the weight of the world no longer sat on his shoulders.

Had coming to Fort Collins banished some of his ghosts?

They listened to the band play for a while, then mutually agreed it was time to go.

When they entered the house, Connor closed the door and looked at her.

"Thanks again," she said brightly. "That was the best meal I've had in ages."

"And you ate enough for two," he teased.

She laughed. "So maybe the baby will grow up with a true appreciation of good Mexican food! Good night."

"Do you have to go to bed right away?"

Dani was taken aback. "Um, I'm a little tired."

"Too sleepy for something to drink?"

"Oh, well, not sleepy, exactly." She hesitated, mesmerized by the glint in his eye.

"I could fix you some herbal tea," he offered, stepping closer, reaching out to unbutton her jacket.

Dani couldn't have moved a step if the house collapsed around them. She was caught in Connor's direct gaze, caught up in the air of anticipation that seemed to cloud her mind.

"That would be nice," she said as she slipped the jacket from her shoulders when he tugged.

He shrugged out of his, dropping both on the nearby chair.

Slowly his head lowered until his lips touched hers, his hands threading through her hair. Giving a sigh, Dani leaned closer, into the kiss she knew she should never accept.

His arms came around her and pulled her against him.

Her own arms seemed to have a life of their own as they encircled his neck, tugging him closer, reveling in the heat that spread like wildfire.

When he deepened the kiss, she forgot about the last time, forgot the hurt, remembered only the glorious feelings that filled her when Connor kissed her.

"Tonight it's you and me, no one else, never anyone else," he said, kissing her again.

She loved Connor Norris.

Not with the airy romantic love she'd thought she felt for Marc, but with her whole being. She loved spending time with him whether he was in a grumpy mood or not. She liked his dry sense of humor, his dedication to work and to the projects under construction. His integrity.

She knew he didn't return her feelings, but she couldn't stop her own any more than she could have stopped that tree from falling on her trailer.

She had two weeks left. She'd make the most of them. And when they parted, she'd have a lifetime to remember him, and love him, and wish him well.

When Dani awoke the next morning, she took her overnight case into the bathroom with her and proceeded to shower and dress. Once that was done, she packed all her things and carried the case with her. They'd be leaving soon.

Where was Connor?

She found him in the kitchen, coffee already prepared, a plate of bagels and cream cheese on the table.

"Good morning."

He rose at the sound of her voice and turned to her. Sweeping her into a kiss, he made her forget everything for a long moment. Then he let her go and winked.

"We need to get going soon," he said.

"I was surprised you didn't pound on the door at four-thirty and demand we leave then."

"I thought you should sleep as long as you could. It's a long drive back."

"Thanks. I'll eat and be ready to go."

Two more weeks and they'd go their separate ways. He'd made that clear to Mick.

But Dani would always have her memories. If they were bittersweet, they were still all hers nonetheless.

Maybe one day she'd tell her baby where the crib had come from and about the man who meant more to Dani than anyone ever had.

She made one last bathroom stop before they departed. When she came out, Connor was on the phone. He hung up.

"That was Mick. He thought I needed an update before we head back."

"Anything wrong?"

"No. Your trailer's being hauled out this morning. The building inspector showed up at eight—a minor miracle, I'd say. And the road in is drying. Here's hoping the storms hold off for a while."

"But we still need to get back."

"Afraid so. Ready?"

She smiled and nodded, hoping he didn't see the effort it cost her.

Things would be different when they returned to the site. He'd be focused on the business at hand. She'd be caught up in trying to decide where to live when the job ended. Their hiatus from real life would be over.

# Chapter Twenty-Three

It was dark by the time Connor eased down the hill to the construction site. He glanced at Dani. She'd been asleep since their last stop, about fifty miles before Carson Creek. They'd had dinner and she'd complained about being tired. How she could sleep through the bumping of the truck on the access road was beyond him. Obviously she was worn out.

He stopped by his trailer and cut the engine. He was tired, too. Driving all day was as exhausting as working a twelve-hour shift.

He looked at the sleeping woman.

How had she come to mean so much to him in so short a time? He'd loved his wife and had sworn never to fall in love again. The pain of losing a loved one was too great.

Yet the protective urge he had around Dani was as unexpected as it was unwelcome. He didn't want to feel connected with anyone. Despite the walls he'd built, she'd breached them.

He was growing to care. And he didn't like the thought.

"Dani, we're home." He shook her shoulder.

When she blinked and opened her eyes, he was startled at the warmth that look brought. Frowning, he pushed away the thought.

"Can you manage?" he asked abruptly. The last thing he wanted was to feel anything. Numbness had a price, but it was worth it to keep pain at bay.

"I'm fine. Wow, I slept all the way?" She looked around, opened her door and slid out.

He got out and picked up their cases from the back of the truck, carrying them to the trailer. Seconds later they were inside.

"I'll head for the office, check on any messages. See you in the morning."

He dropped their bags and headed out faster than was polite. But he was running for his life.

Connor felt like a coward, but was unable to deal with the emotions that were threatening to swamp him. The sooner he got back to work, the sooner things would straighten out and life would go on as it had before Dani arrived.


The next two days were very much as the week before their trip to Fort Collins had been. Connor was gone before she awoke in the morning. He stayed away from the office most of the day. Dinner for Dani on Tuesday was solitary—he ate with Mick.

On Wednesday, he ate quickly and left almost before finishing the last bite.

Dani washed the dishes slowly, wondering what had happened. For one special moment at his parents' home she'd thought they'd drawn closer.

Now it was as if they were back to square one.

If the job wasn't going to end soon, she'd expect him to fire her and get someone else.

Thursday morning, Dani awoke feeling out of sorts. She dressed slowly. Nothing appealed for breakfast. She settled for a banana and some tea. Heading for the office, she was struck by a pain in her abdomen so intense she doubled over, almost falling onto the dirt.

Stunned, she held her stomach, trying to breathe through the pain. She couldn't be going into labor. It was far too soon. She wasn't close to term. But the gripping pain encircled her back and lower abdomen.

Taking a deep breath, she was able to slowly straighten a moment later. Take another deep breath. Three steps later, another sharp pain hit her, starting at her back and moving around to the front, low down and hard.

She moaned with the intensity, sinking to her knees, holding on and hoping she wouldn't scream.

"Dani?" Mick hurried from the office. "Dani, what is it?"

She looked up. "I'm having sharp pains. I can't go into labor. It's not time! What if something's wrong with the baby? Ohh…"

Another pain.

She felt panicky.

She couldn't lose her baby!

Mick scooped her up and carried her to his trailer, rushing inside and placing her gently on the sofa. Two of the men noticed and ran to see if they could assist. He sent them to find Connor. Dialing the hospital, Mick talked to Dani as he waited for someone to answer.

"Hold on, Dani. We'll figure out the best plan and get moving. You're going to be fine and we're not losing that baby!"

The hospital nurse said she should come in immediately, that they'd send an ambulance if needed. By that time Connor had arrived. After one look at Dani, he took the phone from Mick and spoke sharply. "What do we do?"

When the nurse reiterated the option of sending an ambulance, he spoke again. "No, it'll take twice as long that way. We'll bring her in." He hung up and turned to Mick. "What happened?"

"She's having pains. Too early for labor."

Connor crossed swiftly to her and knelt down beside her. "You're going to be okay," he said.

She threw her arms around his neck and clung. "I'm so afraid," she whispered. "Don't let me lose my baby."

"I won't." He picked her up. "Your SUV will be better than the truck," he said to Mick.

"Let's go."

Mick drove, and Connor sat in back with Dani cradled in his arms. When the pains came, he tightened his grip, feeling helpless as he rubbed his hand along her swollen stomach, crooned meaningless words to try to calm her. He was certain this wasn't a normal part of pregnancy, but he didn't want to scare her any more than she was.

Or than he was.

He longed to shout at Mick to drive faster, but the man was already pushing it on the gravel road. Still the moments ticked by slowly. Fear clutched Connor.

Dani sagged against him, cuddling closer, clinging as if he were her lifeline.

"You're going to be all right, you hear?" Connor said softly.

"I'm going to hold you to that," she said.

"Ah, Dani, nothing's going to happen to your baby. You just hang on."

She nodded, closing her eyes. A few moments later another contraction gripped her. Despite his words, Connor saw the fear in her eyes.

He prayed she didn't see it in his.

When they reached Carson Creek's small hospital, Mick drove directly to the emergency entrance. Connor carried Dani inside, where they were met by a nurse who directed them to a nearby cubicle.

A doctor appeared instantly. In seconds, he'd hooked up a fetal monitor and started an IV with medications to stop the contractions. He kept constant, close watch on Dani for a half hour. Connor never left her side, holding her hand while she clung as if she'd never let go.

The contractions gradually slowed, grew less severe and finally stopped.

She was exhausted. Closing her eyes, she seemed to drift off to sleep. Connor gently began to withdraw his hand, but she tightened her grip, her eyes flying open.

"Don't go."

"I'm not going anywhere," he said.

The doctor cleared his throat. "Actually, I want her admitted until we make sure nothing more is going to happen. We'll take her upstairs and get her settled. You can see her again after that. But for now, I'll have to ask you to wait in the reception area."

Connor nodded. He leaned over Dani and brushed her hair back from her face. "I'll see you once you're settled."

She nodded.

Connor's heart was struck at the fear still lingering in her eyes. She tried to smile, but her lips trembled. He kissed her gently, squeezed her hand one last time and turned.

He wanted to smash something, rail against fate. Dani didn't deserve this.

Once outside the curtained area, he stopped, trying to get his emotions under control. He felt as helpless as he had when he'd learned about Catherine and Sammy. There should be something a man could do at times like these.

He walked to the reception area. Mick was sitting with his head bent, elbows resting on his knees, his hands dangling between his legs. He heard Connor and looked up, standing instantly.

"I've been praying. Is she all right?"

"I think she will be. They're admitting her just to make sure. I told her over and over she won't lose the baby, but I don't know that. What if she does, Mick? It'll kill her. She wants that baby in the worst way."

Connor rubbed his chest. He wanted to do something!

"It's a small hospital, but up to date. They'll give her the best they've got," Mick said, gripping Connor's shoulder.

"What if it's not enough?"

"That's out of our hands, boy."

"She asks for so little. Has had so little in life. She needs this baby."

Mick nodded, watching Connor closely. "Maybe you need her," he said.

Connor looked at him. "What does that mean?"

"Love can come in different ways. You and Catherine had a young love, grew up together. But time changes things. It's time you looked around you. You didn't die when Catherine did. Maybe it was because more happiness was in store for you."

"I'm not getting mixed up with anyone again!" Connor reiterated the old litany.

"You already are."

"You're seeing things that aren't there."

"Oh, well, if that's the case, you ready to go back to the site? We can call later and see how she's doing."

Connor stared at Mick, ignoring the twinkle in the older man's eye. "You know I'm not leaving."

"Because you care about her a lot more than you would if Moose or Bill or one of the other men were here. Deny it all you want to the rest of the world, but don't deny it to yourself."

Connor swung away and began to pace the small area.

Mick watched him.

The minutes ticked by. Finally Connor went to the admitting desk.

They'd had long enough to get Dani into her room. He wanted to see her, to make sure she was all right. To make sure she wasn't going to lose that baby.

"Dani Winthrop?" he asked.

The nurse checked the computer monitor. "She's on the second floor. Are you a relative?"

Connor shook his head. "I brought her in. I want to make sure she's all right."

"She's resting. Everything is fine," the nurse said in a soothing tone.

"I want to see her."

"Are you family?"

He shook his head.

"I'm sorry. Only family members are allowed when it's not visiting hours."

She glanced at the clock on the wall. "Visiting hours will be starting at four."

"I want to see her now, not wait until four!"

Connor was not going to be put off by mere technicalities.

"I'm sorry, sir."

Mick joined him. "Problems?"

Connor's frustration threatened to erupt. "Only family are

allowed at non visiting hours."

Mick rocked back and looked at the nurse. "Does a fiancé count as family?" he asked.

"Oh, yes. Are you engaged to Ms. Winthrop?" the nurse asked Connor.

He glanced at Mick, his lips tightening. Where was his resolve when he needed it? He could walk away.

Or run, to avoid becoming entangled with another's life. Avoid the pain and frustration and sadness that life promised.

But he'd also shun any chance of happiness and joy and love.

Who was he kidding?

He could no more walk away from Dani than he could fly to the moon.

"I'm her fiancé," he said.

"Well you should have started off with that," the nurse said. "She's in room 212. The elevators are around the corner."

Connor paused in the doorway to her room. Dani was lying on her side, her back to the door. An IV pole held a solution, the tube snaking down to her arm. Was she asleep? He took a deep breath, his heart twisting at how slight she looked in the standard-issue hospital bed.

It wasn't too late. He saw she was doing all right. He could leave with Mick. Call later to see how she was doing.

He'd been dumb to tell the admitting nurse they were engaged.

Though if he thought about it, it appealed. His lofty ideas of going it alone through life had been destroyed someplace between his week in Pueblo and their visit to Fort Collins.

No matter how he fought against it, he wasn't going to reach that stay-out-of-harm's-way goal he'd set for himself.

He needed to know she would be safe, well, happy. And not just today, but in the future, too.

He wanted to be the one to make sure she stayed safe, well and happy. He wanted to share her days and her nights. See her baby brought safely into the world. Watch the child grow, and watch Dani take joy in teaching her baby all a parent could teach of life's lessons.

For a moment a pang struck as he remembered another little baby, one he'd wanted to teach so much. Sammy's days in the sun had been limited. Dani's baby had its entire life before it.

And it would need a father.

What if it died young?

Connor frowned, rubbing the ache in his chest again. Children were so fragile, so precious.

"What if it lives to be one hundred?" he murmured.

Dani heard him and turned to look over her shoulder. At the sight of her smile, Connor's heart released the last trace of hesitation.

He loved her. And he sure hoped she felt the same.

"Hi," he said, stepping into the room.

"Hi. I thought you and Mick left."

"No. Mick's waiting to hear how you are, then he's heading back to the site. I'm staying."

"Oh, Connor, there's no need. I'm going to be fine. The drip is countering whatever caused the contractions. The doctor said he'd watch me closely for the next couple of days. Once things look stable, I'll be released. But I'm not sure I can return to work."

He lowered the rail on her bed and sat on the side, resting

his palm against the swell of her belly.

"So baby wants to come early, impatient little cuss. Don't worry about work."

Her hand covered his. "You don't have to stay. Go back with Mick. I know there's a lot to do and time's short."

"I hire the best. They can manage without me."

She grinned. "That's not what you said the other day."

"So I like to feel important."

Her smile faded.

"You are important," she said softly. "Thanks for bringing me in. I'm glad I didn't have to come alone in an ambulance."

"I don't want you to ever have to do anything alone," he said.

"I won't, once the baby comes. As long as it comes when it's supposed to."

"I was thinking more along the lines of an adult, not just your baby. Maybe you should get married."

"Oh, yeah, like that's going to happen," she scoffed. "Besides, I've sworn off men, don't you remember?"

"So maybe you should consider changing your mind and swearing off every other man in the world."

"Every *other* man?"

"Except me."

She stared at him.

He raised her hand to his lips and brushed a kiss across her palm.

"Marry me, Dani. Let me be your husband, lover, father to your baby. Father to babies of our own."

She blinked and shook her head. "I think the drugs are causing hallucinations."

He tightened his grip. This wasn't easy.

And it wasn't going the way he'd thought it would. Why didn't she throw herself into his arms and tell him yes?

Instead her look grew wary. "I thought you loved Catherine," she said.

"I did. I think I loved her from the time we were in fourth grade. But she's gone. I won't lie and say I can forget her. I won't ever do that. But she'll never come between us, I promise you that!"

Dani tugged on her hand, but he refused to release her.

"I thought you wanted no involvement. That after the project closed for the winter, we'd not see each other again. Wasn't that the reason for the hasty trip to Fort Collins to get the crib? So you wouldn't have to see me after we shut down?"

He nodded, his gaze steadfast and calm. "Or so I thought. But it was as if visiting Fort Collins released me from a prison cell of my own making. It's a nice town where a bad thing happened. But I didn't crash and burn when I went back. In fact, I enjoyed showing you my hometown. I wanted you to like it so you'd settle there. Then when I went home to visit my folks, I could stop by and see you."

"Huh?"

"But today put paid to that notion. I can't wait for occasional visits. I wanted to avoid entanglements. I never wanted to feel again the pain losing Catherine and Sammy brought. But today was worse. You were in pain, in danger of losing your baby, and I was totally helpless. I realized then that I was involved, entangled and about as wrapped up as a person could be. I was devastated when Catherine died, but you know what? I wouldn't trade the years we had for anything. I would have given my life for her and Sammy—but I wasn't given that choice. So unless I hide in a monastery, there's no avoiding life—fears, pain, loss and all."

He kissed her hand again and leaned forward until he filled her vision.

"But there's all that joy that also comes with living," he said. "And you bring me an abundant measure of that."

Tears welled up in her eyes. "And the baby? Can you accept my baby, too?"

"Yes, Dani. I will cherish your baby. Sammy taught me how to be a father. I'll be the best dad I can for your baby. Our baby. And maybe we'll have more. Take a chance on me, my love. Marry me."

"Love?" she whispered, touching his cheek with her free hand, her other gripping his tightly.

"I love you, Dani Winthrop. I want you in my life for as long as either of us has. I'm not going to run off when things get tough. I'd never abandon you or the baby. I want the chance to love you for all time."

He held her gaze with his as tension rose even higher. She had to say yes!

"Oh, Connor, I love you so much!" She flung her arm around his neck and pulled him closer to kiss him.

He responded, releasing her hand to enfold her in his arms. She was soft and sweet—and his. Her response had been exactly what he'd hoped for. He loved her. And Dani loved him.

A monitor sounded. A nurse dashed into the room, stopping when she saw the couple break apart guiltily.

"Heart rate increased dramatically," she said dryly, coming to take Dani's pulse. "But I don't think in this instance it's a cause for alarm."

"We're getting married," Dani said happily.

The nurse raised an eyebrow and glanced at her patient's

stomach. "Not a moment too soon," she murmured.

Dani giggled, exchanging a loving look with Connor.

"I agree," he said, winking at her.

Epilogue


"Push!" Connor urged his wife, as he supported her in the birthing room in the Fort Collins hospital. It was a snowy day in early December, the perfect day for a baby to be born.

"I am pushing," she panted, straining to give birth.

She rested a moment and looked over her shoulder at the man she loved.

"If you don't like the way I'm doing this, you take over," she snapped.

Connor kissed her cheek. "You're doing perfectly. No one could do better. I'm the coach, remember?"

She pushed as another contraction hit and slowly the baby moved down the birth canal.

"A bouncing baby girl," the doctor said, receiving the infant. She handed her to a nurse, who wrapped the baby in a blanket and laid her on Dani's stomach. Connor and Dani gazed at the tiny girl with a mop of curly brown hair. The baby's eyes opened and she blinked, her little chest rising and falling as she gazed solemnly around.

Connor reached out a finger and caressed her cheek.

"We have a daughter," he said. "And she's as beautiful as her mother."

"Did you want a son?" Dani asked, hoping he wouldn't be disappointed.

"Maybe next time." He kissed her gently. "Hello, Mommy."

Next time maybe a boy. Or the time after that. Dani didn't

care. She wanted to fill their home with the laughter of children, and share the rich bounty of love Connor brought. This precious baby was only the first. They had both agreed on that.

"I love you," she said, tears flowing. How could one woman bear so much happiness?

"I love you, Dani Norris. You and our little Melanie Elizabeth."

She smiled and touched the baby, rejoicing in her birth. They were a family of three now.

Dani had no fears that Connor still longed for his first wife. He'd shown her in every way that she was his love, his life and his future. She was sure he still thought about Catherine sometimes. And it was only right he do so. She'd been an important part of his life. The mother of his first child. Nothing would ever take that away.

Dani was grateful he'd let himself fall in love again—with her. She knew their future would continue to be wonderful—full of love and happiness. She had no reason to fear the past, only look to the future—their future.

Mick was in the waiting room, as were her new in-laws. Everyone awaited word of the new baby. There would be celebration and rejoicing that Connor and Dani had a beautiful baby girl.

Dani fit right in with the Norris family, amazed at the closeness of family who loved each other. Amazed at how they welcomed her into their midst.

She was constantly surprised at how easily her husband showed his love. He was still the tough, demanding, no-excuse boss on the job site, but behind their closed door, he was as tender and romantic as any woman could wish.

She glanced up and caught her breath. Would she ever lose

this wondrous feeling around him?

He leaned over and kissed her. They had restrained themselves to just kisses for several weeks. And there would be several more to go before they could make love again, but she could hardly wait. He thrilled her to her toes, and probably always would.

Connor brushed the baby's downy hair. "In another year or two, we should try for another one. Maybe a boy next time, what do you think?"

She smiled, her heart filled to bursting. There was no greater gift he could have given her. The past was truly behind them both. The future was bright with promise.

I hope you enjoyed **Sweet *Meant To Be*** If so, would you be so kind as to leave a review at the vendor where you purchased it? Reviews can be long or short, they are always a help. Thank you.

# More books by Barbara McMahon

**The Harts of Texas Series**
Rebel Heart
Tangled Hearts
Reckless Heart

**Cowboy Heroes Series**
Blue Bells on the Hill
Cowboy's Bride
One Stubborn Cowboy
Crazy About a Cowboy
Never Doubt a Cowboy
Cowboy Marshal
Summer Cowboy
Second Chance Cowboy
Movie Star Cowboy

**Tropical Escape Series**
Island Rendezvous
Come into the Sun
Island Paradise
Destination Romance Boxed Set

**Rocky Point Series**
The Family Next Door
Rocky Point Reunion
Rocky Point Promise
Rocky Point Hero

**Elite Security Mystery Series**
Trusting Jake

**The Ultimate Billionaires**
The Cynical Sheikh
Falling for the Sheikh
A Sheikh of Her Own
The Unforgettable Sheikh

**Other Books**
A Soldier's Christmas
I'll Take Forever
Jared's Promise
The Paper Marriage
The Christmas Locket
The Banished Bride
Cowboy Charade
The Cowboy's Special Christmas
Mail Order Bride
Because of You
Sweet Meant To Be

www.ingramcontent.com/pod-product-compliance
Lightning Source LLC
Chambersburg PA
CBHW051639260626
47170CB00004B/1244